DEATH & CHAOS

CHAOS AT POLYTECH UNIVERSITY

BOOK ONE

CASSANDRA JOY
G.R. LOREWEAVER

Published by Saucy Pineapple Publishing 2022

Ebook ISBN: 978-1-957592-16-9

Paperback ISBN: 978-1-957592-17-6

10 9 8 7 6 5 4 3 2

To the fans and supporters of our #MondayMadness. Thank you all!

A NOTE FROM THE AUTHORS

If you're a fan of Cassandra's Neighborhood series, be warned that though this series will end with a HEA, it is not wrapped up and tied with a neat bow in this book. Or the next couple. Be aware that you will have to get through a lot of chaos to get to the happy.

If you're a fan of G.R.'s Noctifer Witch series or have spent much time following #MondayMadness, this will not be a surprise to you. What you might find surprising is just how twisted this particular road is going to get. Hang in there. We promise it'll be worth it in the end.

While this is a slow-burn for reverse harem, there is plenty of sex right from the beginning. If MM isn't your thing, don't worry. The sex with Prescilla is coming. Eventually.

There is BDSM. There's a sexual predator. There is drug and alcohol abuse. There is… death. Shocking, we know, since it's in the title. Do not panic when a member of the harem dies!!

There are also Easter eggs and jokes and puns and sarcasm galore, just like you'd expect from #JoyWeaver. There is passion and food and sex and food and awkward conversations and food and heartache and food. All the good things you crave from us.

We hope you enjoy this first series co-written by us. More to come. So much more in store.

PROLOGUE

$\mathscr{I}$ sneered at the disgusting people around me.

I didn't want to be here. I *hated* it here.

Unfortunately, this was my punishment. Whether or not I'd earned it? That was debatable.

I cracked my neck as I glanced around this new campus. It looked just like all the others.

PolyTech University.

The mascot was a gryphon, but it looked puny against the PTU shield. I chuckled at the thought that any gryphon could hope to go up against me… and win. I'd had gryphons for breakfast more times than I could count. Not that any of these red and white babies could possibly pass for the real thing.

I was sure this would be *just* like all of the other colleges. Full of stupid young people determined to either drink themselves to death or study themselves brain dead.

Partying could be fun. And I *did* enjoy fun. But if you had no other ambitions, then you were beneath my acknowledgement. I also had no qualms about gaining knowledge and immersing yourself in your education. After all, you never find stupid people in charge–at least not for long.

1

You can however, find smart people doing stupid things. Hence my current predicament.

If only my love would have paid more attention to me, then I would not have sought out comfort in the arms of another. Of course *he* couldn't be punished–stupid fucking falcon–so my love took out his wrath on me instead. I didn't blame him though. His vengeance was one of the many things I loved about him. And yes, I did still love him. So very deeply.

So what would I do now?

Well, I had been playing nice for quite some time. A millennia, really. Maybe that should come to an end. I wanted to have some of my own fun. My personal brand. If being good wouldn't get my love to notice me, then maybe a little havoc would. That thought alone had my nipples peak to attention. Mmmm... Havoc.

I watched the tidy, little students walking around the neat, little campus and smiled to myself. Yes, this place could certainly go for a little disarray. Just a little... chaos.

I inhaled deeply and smelled the uniqueness pungent in the air, and my smile grew. What a delicious twist that would be.

Oh yes, this was the perfect place for me to be right now.

I shifted my foot slightly and tripped a student walking past. When they hit the ground with a thud, pure glee washed across my face and through my veins.

What could I say?

I was the Eater of Hearts. Devourer of the Dead. The Swallower. And I *thrived* in the chaos.

1

PRESCILLA BENNETT

I looked up and around the neighborhood.

It was a decent little community.

Kids were riding bikes up and down the road. And a man down at the end of the block was mowing his lawn while a lady walked her pomeranian across the street from me.

I waved at the woman then turned to go into the new house.

My parents had decided to move halfway across the country just because I said I wanted to go to PolyTech University. It had one of the best art programs in the world, after all. I knew they trusted me, and it wasn't like they needed the small discount in-state tuition would give them.

No, they just want to be near me.

Because they liked me.

Maybe if I'd had a sibling, they wouldn't have been *quite* so... hovery.

A secret part of me that would never admit it was thrilled that they liked being near me. That they liked spending time with me. That we were still close even though I was an adult now.

Because I did know families that didn't get along. Where the kids hated their manipulative parents.

3

I really had lucked out in the parent lottery.

So here I was, a freshman at college, and totally moving into a new house with my moms. No dorm. No rental house. No roommates. Just a girl and her two moms. And if my dad had his way, another set of parents in no time at all.

I was only two when my mom informed my dad that she was bi and in love with another woman, Charlene Thoreau. Turns out he'd been having an affair with his cyber security expert Olivia.

I can't remember whether or not the divorce at the time was amicable, because from the time I could remember anything, they'd both already remarried, and I had three moms and one dad. They never lived far away from each other so that they could all happily parent me as a team, and they really did enjoy spending time together still.

While my Dad, Cornelius Bennett, and Olivia, aka Mum the Third, were still living back home in Louisiana, I knew my dad was trying to rearrange their lives to move here.

Did I mention that I really love my parents, but that they can be a little… clingy?

"Did you get the box with your pillow in it?" my mom asked from the doorway. See what I mean?

I couldn't help smiling at her, though. Loretta Thoreau had always been one of the most beautiful women I had ever known. She kept her black hair in long braids, like mine, but always had them gathered into a ponytail at the back.

We looked so similar that there had been a few occasions when someone would mistake us for sisters. Yeah, it's not flattering to be mistaken for the same age as your mother, even *if* she looked younger than twice my age.

The one big difference was our eyes. Where mine were a deep chocolate, hers were dark caramel, and always full of so much love.

Remembering that she asked me a question, I reached forward and gave her hand a gentle squeeze as I answered.

"Yep! It's got all of my bedding, so I'll be able to sleep on my bed tonight." I gave her a bright smile, one last squeeze, and then continued past her to the bedroom over the garage.

The room had an extra large bay window that let a lot of sunlight in to reflect off the butter yellow walls, casting the whole room in a delicately soft glow. I had considered repainting it. After all, yellow had never been my favorite color, but once the sun streamed in, that yellow really was perfect.

My favorite part of the room was still that enormous window.

With a window that large, you'd think it would face the front of the house, but it didn't. It faced the back yard and a good chunk of the next door neighbor's yard. I didn't mind that one bit. It felt like it offered me a lot more privacy without having to sacrifice the natural light by adding in thick curtains.

I glanced out the window and took in the scene. Our yard was simple and could use a little love, but I knew that Momma Charlene would be revitalizing it in no time.

I let my attention drift as I looked around the neighbor's backyard. That yard had a large pool with a hot tub inset at one end.

And three, gorgeous, nearly naked men lounging around it…

There might have been a patio? Some trees and flowers? I wasn't really sure since I couldn't drag my attention away from the eye candy.

Two of the men looked to be twins, though their tattoos didn't quite match up. Big biker twins. Dark hair, dark eyes, and dark golden skin. And, oh baby… I wanted to lick those washboard abs. I just wanted to be the center of a twin sandwich. Take them both at the same time. Be bracketed by those huge thighs and huger biceps.

Yep, huger is a word, I just decided.

Because no other word goes with those delicious arms.

And the third guy?

Talk about the sexy, mysteriously dark vampire I've always dreamed of! Yum.

His pale skin practically glistened in the sun's rays, though not quite diamond sparkles like that one book. Because that's ridiculous. His soft brown hair fell in waves around his lean shoulders.

His hands were long and lean, and I couldn't stop myself from wondering what they would feel like caressing my skin… or wrapped around my throat.

One of the twins looked up at me, smiling. I gave an embarrassed little wave, then backed away from the window. Just enough that they wouldn't be able to see me in the shadows but still close enough that I could look down into their yard and admire their… swimsuits.

I licked my lips as Mr. Pale Perfect dove into the pool at the deep end. When he came back up, his hair was slicked back to frame his handsomely angular face. I watched as water droplets slid down his sculpted chest. It was smooth without any hair, but glistened.

Did I mention the glistening?

Something shiny caught my eye and I squinted a little. Trying to get a better look.

What was this shiny little speck right at his nip–

Oh! Oh… oh my. He had his nipples pierced. I wondered if he had any *other* piercings. I might have licked my lips again at the idea of discovering all his body modifications.

One of the biker twins, the one that'd smiled at me, sat up and straddled the lounge he'd been lying on. He leaned forward, saying something to his twin. Then he stood and squatted next to the pool to kiss the vampire-look-alike on the lips. It was a scorching kiss; I could feel the heat even from up here. Then he turned to walk into their house.

As I watched, the other biker twin stood up, looked up at my window, and then put his fingers in his mouth to whistle. I slowly stepped forward and opened the window.

"Yo, babe," he yelled up at me. "Get your gorgeous ass down here so that we can meet properly!" He was swiveling his hips and thrusting them up at me like he honestly thought that was being sexy or something.

My lip curled up in disgust. "I don't think so, asshole!" I yelled back. I slammed my window closed and turned to make my bed.

Such a jerk! A gorgeous jerk, yes. But a complete and utter asshole.

No one tells me what to do.

Once my bed was all settled, I headed downstairs to have dinner with all four of my parents before Dad and Mum the Third headed back to Louisiana in the morning.

2

JACKSON MILLER

This was the last straw.

I could not believe my egotistical idiot of a brother. Catcalling the new neighbor. Like she was a hooker instead of a nice girl.

Bet he wouldn't have done that if he'd seen the man helping them move in earlier. At least, I hoped not.

Who was I kidding? Of course he would. He actually thought he was irresistible.

I hated the way he treated all women. And I certainly didn't want him living next to a house full of them.

But truly, this was my tipping point. I could only handle so much financial irresponsibility and general narcissism. Then to be rude to the neighbor too?

Enough.

"If you're not going to pay your part of the rent, why should we even bother letting you live with us?" I asked. "You never clean up after yourself. You eat all of our food without contributing to the grocery budget. You haven't paid the electric bill like you said you would. I can't take this anymore, Jonathan. I'm done. You're going to have to find somewhere else to live."

"Are you kicking me out?" Jonathan stared at me like I'd grown a second head. "I'm your brother! Your twin?! And you are kicking me out of the house that we *share*?"

"Yes!" I yelled. "It's bad enough that Cary and I have to put up with your lazy ass, but now you're harassing our neighbor! And let's get real here, Jonathan. The rental agreement is in *my* name, so I can do whatever I want."

"You're kicking me out because of the new bitch next door?!"

"No," I ground my teeth. "I'm kicking you out because you've not been paying any of your bills or doing a single damn thing around here to contribute. Your being an asshole to the neighbor is just where I'm finally drawing the line."

He threw up his hands and stormed toward the front door. "Whatever, man. You know what? Fuck you. Fuck you both!" And with a slam of the door, he was gone.

Good riddance, Asshole.

"So, should we start packing up all of his stuff?" Cary asked, rubbing his hands together in a far too excited gesture. "Maybe dump it all on the front lawn like a cheesy rom-com movie?"

I started laughing and pulled him into my arms. "No, we're not going to decorate our lawn with his junk. But packing him up? Yeah. Let's start that."

"What are we going to do about making the rent?" Cary looked up at me with soft brown eyes. "We can't exactly afford it with just the two of us. Even if he rarely pulled his weight, at least it was something."

"We'll think of something," I kissed him on the nose. "Know anyone that needs a room even though the semester is starting on Monday?"

"Um, let me check with my lab partner from last semester," Cary grinned at me. "I swear he lives in the library."

I laughed and kissed Cary again. He made my soul sing.

This time the kiss was on the lips and much deeper. It didn't take long for my cock to harden and beg to be let loose. I broke off the kiss and began pulling Cary toward my bedroom.

I was definitely going to enjoy the taste of my boyfriend tonight. I needed him.

And not just because seeing the new girl's smile earlier had turned me on.

Nope.

Not. At. All.

Cary chuckled like he knew exactly what I was thinking. But then a purr came from his chest, and I knew he was going to enjoy me just as much.

Once we were in my room, he shoved the door closed and gently pushed me to the bed. "I want to ride you," he murmured.

I grinned, stripping my shirt off and shoving my shorts and boxers down. I loved when Cary went all dominant male on me. Outside of the bedroom, everyone assumed that because I was taller and broader and had all the tattoos that I would be the Dom.

After all, while Cary was gregarious, I had the more commanding personality.

At least, outside of the bedroom.

But once it was just the two of us, it was almost like a switch flipped. 'Cary The Dom' showed up, and I willingly gave up control. He could turn my brain off and help me actually relax like nothing and nobody else could.

Once Cary's clothes had disappeared somewhere, he shoved me back onto the bed and crawled up to straddle me. He grabbed my cock as he leaned forward and began whispering in my ear.

Almost immediately, I shuddered at his contact.

What did he whisper?

I hadn't the slightest clue.

It really didn't matter.

What mattered was that his breath ghosted across my skin. That one of his hands roamed my chest and shoulders and arm. That the other pulled on me slowly as I thickened and throbbed in his palm. That his thighs held my hips tight. That his hair fell on either side of our faces, cloaking us in our own little world.

He was everything.

He was the *only* thing.

Just as I thought that I couldn't handle any more teasing because I needed to come, he shifted his weight to grab a bottle of lube off my nightstand. Within seconds he'd slicked me up, and I couldn't help but moan.

He reached back to prep his own hole and the sight of him playing with himself nearly undid me. My man was so sexy. I got so lost watching his fingers that I didn't realize he was smirking at me until his voice came out in a low rumble, "Like what you see, rockstar?"

I laughed at the nickname but then licked my lips while I nodded. "Want in you," I managed to get out.

"Oh, you will be," he said. Then he slid his fingers in even further and curled them just right. A look of bliss came over his face when he twigged his prostate.

I loved that look. I loved that peace and happiness took him over. That his cares all fell away. It was even better when he actually came.

"Cary," I groaned.

Why was he torturing me? Playing with himself but not letting me in him? I craved having him sink onto me, having his warmth engulf me.

A pleased little sound came from the back of Cary's throat as he pulled his fingers out. "If you're not patient, I'll make you wait longer," he murmured.

When I nearly choked on air at that thought, he winked at me. Then he slicked up my cock one more time. "Do you think I could make you come just like this? Holding you and not letting you fuck me?"

I moaned in frustration. "I'll do whatever you'd like, Cary!"

There was no other answer.

I knew it.

He would make good on his threat if I didn't admit it.

"Such a good boy," Cary purred.

He leaned towards me, bracing both of his hands on my pecs, then shifted forward so that my dick popped free from between us and ended up right next to his entrance. He paused then, just drawing out the anticipation. It took everything in me not to beg him.

When he finally sank down on me, both of us let out moans of pleasure from deep in our chests. There was nothing that felt as good as being joined to Cary. And it didn't really matter who was throwing and who was catching.

As long as the two of us were together, it was heaven.

After a minute of just enjoying being joined together, he began to move to a slow, sensuous rhythm.

He really was trying to torture me.

"I'm not *trying* to torture you," he chuckled. Had I said that out loud? "I'm succeeding," he continued with a smirk.

I couldn't stop my laugh from bursting out of me.

I reached up to hold onto his hips, but he swatted my hands away. I bit my lip, trying to hide my smile. He sometimes got into a "no touchy!" mood in bed. It was a Dom thing.

As if reading my thoughts, he grabbed my wrists and crossed them above my head. "Stay," he said.

Then he lowered his face to my neck and really picked up the pace. I grabbed the pillow in both hands and held on tight.

Cary nuzzled into my neck, breathing deeply. He drove himself down onto me over and over like a blood-pumping piston at full speed. As I quickly neared my peak, I gripped the pillow even tighter, trying to keep myself from coming before Cary said I could.

When I thought I couldn't hold out anymore, Cary growled, "Come," into my shoulder.

I fell apart.

He arched back, my orgasm triggering his. He cried out my name as his release splashed all over my chest and neck.

I couldn't stop myself. I let go of the pillow to reach up and tweak one of the piercings in his nipples. A shiver ran down his spine, and then he leaned back down. Without any hesitation, he pressed our chests together and began kissing me slowly again.

CASSANDRA JOY & G.R. LOREWEAVER

"We should wash up," I murmured. As much as I loved being soaked in his come, I didn't like when it dried on me.

"I'm not finished with you yet," Cary whispered back. "I bet I can get another three or four orgasms out of you tonight."

I laughed and grabbed his ass, pulling his hips even closer to mine. "I'm not sure my refractory time is quite that good."

"Oh, it is," he said with a smirk. "Remember that one time…"

I laughed and covered his mouth with my own. My dick twitched before it could fully exit his ass. Yeah, he might be right. We might have gone all night long more than a time or two. He was just too damn sexy.

And I loved my man.

3

CARY CARPENTER

I wound my way through the stacks, looking for Guillermo "Meemo" Pérez.

The dude was a studious guy. I was pretty sure the only reason I'd passed Chem last semester was because he was my partner. He had a way of explaining things so that they actually made sense.

His brains were so damn sexy.

As I navigated the shelves and tables, I felt people turning to stare after me.

Flirtatious glances. Bit lips. Increased breathing.

Geez. I couldn't even walk through here without dozens of people wanting me. It was fun to bask in the attention sometimes. But some days, like today, I had something I actually wanted to accomplish. And all of the sultry looks were just annoying.

As I suspected, I found Meemo at a red lacquered study table tucked into the very back of the Science and Technology floor. I wasn't kidding when I told Jack that I thought Meemo lived here. This table might as well have his name engraved on it right next to the inlaid gold PTU gryphon.

"Yo, Meemo," I said as I plopped into a chair across from him. "Did you ever find a place, or did you finally decide to move into the library?" I stretched out my legs, and one calf brushed along the outside of his leg.

He slowly looked up and blinked owlishly at me through his glasses.

I could see that his brain was trying to switch gears, and I wondered how long he'd been studying. The semester wouldn't even start until Monday, but he was probably trying to read all of his textbooks before classes started.

Like I said: studious.

And, hell, that sleepy blink was sexy as fuck.

"Hey, Cary," he said, licking his lips and rubbing the back of his neck. "Um, yeah. I've not really been able to find something I can afford."

"How's $500 a month, utilities included, sound?" I asked with a grin.

He blinked slowly again. Processing. "That'd be great. Especially if it's close to campus. It's not out in the middle of nowhere, is it? Or one of those party houses, right?"

"Nah," I chuckled. "And no giant blow-up gryphon in the front yard on game days. It's a block off of campus. My boyfriend's brother just moved out, so it's just the two of us, and we've got an empty room. We cover most of it, just need a little extra help."

"Yeah," Meemo's face lit up. "That sounds great! Um... your boyfriend?"

"Haven't I told you about Jackson?" I asked. "We've been together for... ages."

"Oh," Meemo blinked. "No you hadn't. I can't wait to meet him." He looked back down at his book, dismissing me. But I caught how his hands had clenched for a second when I'd said *boyfriend.*

I was pretty sure Meemo was straight as could be, but that didn't stop thoughts of him in my bed floating through my brain. The boy was serious eye candy.

Yummy.

Wait, was the reaction because he was attracted to me too?

Nah. I waved the thought away.

"Come by tomorrow afternoon," I said, writing the address down on a corner of his notebook. "We should have the asshole out of the house by then."

"What… happened?" Meemo tilted his head to look at me. "Are you kicking him out?"

"Oh yeah," I nodded. "A new family moved in next door. Gorgeous girl about our age, with her two moms. And Jack's brother wolf-whistled at her. Thrusted his hips like he wanted to screw her into the ground." I shook my head. I mean, *I* had wanted to screw her into the ground, but Jonathan had just been so crass about it. "It doesn't sound so bad, but really it was just the last thing that happened. He's been a pain in the ass our entire lives. If he weren't Jack's twin, I probably would have killed him by sixth grade."

Meemo laughed nervously. "So… I can stay as long as I don't yell at the neighbors?"

He licked those plump lips again.

Damn, that was distracting.

"No," I grinned. "You can stay as long as you pay the rent. Seriously, there were tons of reasons we've been needing to kick Jonathan out. He's a total ass. It won't be hard to be a better roommate than he is."

"Okay," Meemo nodded. "I'll make sure all of my stuff is in my car."

I paused for a second as a thought struck me. "Were you planning on living in your car the whole semester?"

"Well," he shifted in his seat. "I figured I'd eventually find something."

Oh, man.

"Meemo…" I sighed and pinched the bridge of my nose. "I wish you'd told me. Even if we hadn't kicked Jonathan out today, we would have let you live with us. I wouldn't have wanted you living out of your car. I could have moved into Jack's room. I have no idea why we've got separate rooms as it is." I rolled my eyes dramatically, but Meemo didn't laugh.

"Okay," he whispered. "I'll remember that next time I'm homeless." He loosed a small grin then, and I burst out laughing.

"Alright, man." I stood. "Don't wait for tomorrow; come over tonight. We'll get you set up."

After he waved, I turned and left the campus library, avoiding the groups of girls who had started to follow me through the rooms.

Meemo would be a thousand times better than Jonathan.

4

PRESCILLA BENNETT

I flopped face down on the freshly made sheets with a deep sigh.

Between the wonderfully clean linen smell of my bedspread and the incredibly full belly, I was well on my way to a food coma.

I shouldn't have been surprised by tonight's feast.

One of the things my moms enjoyed most was cooking together, and I knew they couldn't wait to break in that new kitchen.

Dinner was glorious. They made some of my favorites: cajun shrimp salad, parmesan noodles with asparagus, and lemon raspberry mini tarts. My moms were beasts in the kitchen, and the foodgasm that came with that first bite was enough to prove it.

Mum the Third was pretty decent around a turkey sandwich, but Dad?

Well… he could mess up those canned SpaghettiOs kids loved.

I still couldn't look at those cans at the store without shuddering from my last memory of him cooking.

Never again.

I flipped to my back and sighed again. I was so glad I changed into comfy clothes before dinner, because I didn't think the skinny jeans I had on earlier would be able to be buttoned right now.

The tiny pooch of my fullness almost pulled my t-shirt out further than my breasts. That thought was slightly irritating.

It wasn't that my girls were small. They fully filled a B cup. But whenever I got bloated, I might as well be flat-chested for all they showed. At least I could always count on my hips and ass for sex appeal.

Not that I really cared much about my sex appeal.

Oh I thought about sex plenty, but actually getting there? Well, that never seemed high on my priorities.

Now don't get me wrong. I was no "innocent" little flower. I had fooled around plenty, and had a nice pair of vibrating panties that helped relieve some frustrations.

Just no actual intercourse.

Yet.

I hadn't met the right person.

Yeah.

That's what I would just keep telling myself.

A light shone through the window and pulled my attention away from thoughts of finding those wonderful little panties.

I moved to the window and saw that the neighbors were in the backyard. It was getting darker, but not terribly late yet. I could see the pale beauty and the non-asshole biker, but it was the third guy that captured my full attention.

He had a dark and brooding look about him but with this air of intelligence. His black faux-hawk was slicked back, amping up his sex appeal. He'd been built wider in the shoulders and hips than the biker, but I knew it had to be pure muscle.

Looking at him sent shivers down my spine and my nipples pebbled under my thin shirt.

He reached up and pushed his glasses up his nose, before turning his line of sight directly toward me. As if he knew I was watching him, secretly wishing for his attention.

I froze under his pointed gaze. My heart pounded wildly in my chest.

Neither of us moved.

I felt exposed, naked all the way to my soul, and I had this deep, primal need to go to him.

He parted his lips, and the sudden fear that he might ask me to come to him had me closing my curtains quickly.

I turned back to my bed, but instead of walking towards it, I simply slid to the floor on far too weak legs.

I was already feeling unsure about the neighbors next door. But this guy?

No one had ever called to me so *deeply* before.

I scrubbed my hands across my face and tried to calm my still racing heart.

How was it possible for a man to be *that* attractive?

That body was all power, and I couldn't help but yearn to have my hands on it.

Or better yet, to have his hands on me. No... all of him on me.

I'd bet he was an amazing lover. There was no way a guy looked like that and didn't know his way around a woman's body.

I had a deep appreciation for that sort of experience, but for some reason, this time I had also been hit with an intense surge of jealousy. I didn't want him touching other women. And I sure as hell didn't want them touching him!

Woah...

Easy girl. Getting a little ahead of yourself there, Prescilla.

Except my brain was stuck on a repeating cycle, and his was the only image that played.

I closed my eyes and let his features come more vividly into my mind.

Those slightly pouty lips looked so inviting when he'd opened his mouth. What I wouldn't give to have that mouth on me. Kissing me. A little nibble here, maybe a bite there. Then he would move down and slick his tongue right up my–

Wow...

Alright!

I bounced off the floor and headed to the nearest box labeled "PB Privates" and snickered. Mom fancied herself a comedian.

I was pretty sure this was the box that all of my more *personal* items were packed into.

Time to find those panties because there was no way I was going to be able to relax tonight without them.

Not one bit.

5

GUILLERMO PÉREZ

I tried not to pout when she closed the curtains.

My padré always said that 'real' men don't pout.

My line of thinking must have made me scowl though because Cary snagged my attention.

"What's eating you, big guy?" he asked, before following my gaze in the direction of her window.

He looked back at me with a smirk on his face. "Ah, I see you've noticed our rather enticing new neighbor." He added an eyebrow wiggle, and I couldn't help rolling my eyes at him.

I scrubbed my hand down my face but met his scrutinizing gaze and relented.

"Yeah. I saw her. She's pretty, but I have to focus on school. I have a scholarship, and girls only complicate things." He knew I was lying, just like I knew that I wouldn't be able to get the thought of her out of my mind.

Jackson chimed in, "That's probably best. I mean, things would be awkward getting involved with a neighbor, right? Even if she is really pretty."

Cary chuckled and nudged him with his elbow. "Jack, you

dirty dog. I knew I wasn't the only one pining over those big brown eyes."

Jackson smiled at Cary, and I could see the love shining in his eyes. They stared at each other for a moment, before I interrupted them with a small cough.

"Well, I am going to head to my room and get my sheets put on. Maybe dive into more suggested reading for my Historical Perspectives class. Besides, you two seem like you could use some alone time." I polished off the last of my beer and stood up to head into the house.

Cary and Jackson were busy whispering to each other the way my grandparents used to. I wondered if they realized how in love they truly were.

I barely made it past them before Cary stopped me with his hand on my arm.

He smiled and said, "Welcome home, Meemo. I think we will all get along just fine here together. I can understand if you are missing that feeling that comes from having a big family at your back, but Jack and I are here for you."

I nodded to him and headed inside.

I appreciated Cary's words. I was not built to thrive in a solo environment, and he knew it. The fact that he offered both him and Jackson as my new family of sorts set my nerves at ease a bit more.

Setting my bottle in the recycling bin, I only made it halfway down the hall before a vision assaulted me.

Her pouty lips parted open slightly. Her back arching with pleasure.

I inhaled deeply and swore I could smell her. She smelled like honey and apples. The scent made my mouth water, and I couldn't help but imagine how she would taste. How it would feel to run my hands through those tiny velvet braids. Just give them a small tug while my hand explored–

My eyes snapped open, and I panted heavily, leaning against the wall. I wasn't sure when I closed my eyes, but when I looked down, I groaned at the sight of dampness spreading across the front of my sweats.

Fuck!

I pushed off the wall, spared a brief moment to snag a change of shorts and towel, and then slipped quickly into the bathroom. Once I freed my sensitive skin from my irritating clothes, I jumped under the cold spray of the shower.

I shivered a little, but I didn't dare turn up the temperature of the water. I needed it cold. The colder the better because, apparently, I was some little creeper who came in his pants at the sight of a pretty girl.

As my thoughts shifted back to her, my liberated–if chilly– cock began to twitch to life again, I groaned and rested my head on the tile.

So much for calming things down.

I gripped my painfully hard cock tightly in my grasp. Almost punishing myself. But the small amount of pain did nothing to quell the fire that had started building again.

How the hell was I going to live next to a woman like *that* and keep my focus?

I hoped moving in here was a good choice because I had a feeling junior year was going to go by twice as slowly.

6

GRAYSON LEBLANC

I arranged my brushes for the millionth time, hoping that it would jiggle some inspiration loose.

Classes started tomorrow, and I was officially a senior. Woohoo!

Four days until my first submission for my senior art portfolio was due, and I had... nothing.

It was a prerequisite for this final Advanced Color Applications class.

I stared at a blank canvas. Just like I had been for over a month now.

Why, you ask? My inspiration was gone.

Not lacking.

Not stunted.

Just... *gone*.

I had always seen the world in a wide array of colors with an endless palette and unlimited potential.

Until a month ago...

My whole life, it had just been my mom and me. She was a magnificent creature, always so full of life. She was also my biggest fan. And I didn't just mean that she doted on the stick figures I drew as a toddler. No, she was an art curator and knew her stuff.

That's why I would always preen when she said she liked this piece or another. Her compliments were genuine and not biased. Because she was also never afraid to tell me when something sucked.

Okay, maybe not that harsh since she was my mom, but she never danced around telling me when a piece needed more work or when a skill needed more fine tuning.

We were told the cancer was in remission.

Apparently, that didn't last.

She had already lost both breasts in the hopes of cutting the disease out of her. That alone had taken so much spark away from her. But when we went in for that check-up and got the news that not only was it back, but that it was very aggressive, she lost all hope.

It drained out of her in a single afternoon.

Her health declined almost as quickly as her spirits, and I had no sooner accepted her diagnosis before she was just… *gone*.

Saying it'd been hard was like saying that a hurricane was just a little rain.

Losing her wrecked me.

I had this immense feeling like nothing "fit" anymore.

I sold the house here in Polyville because it felt way too big and retreated to my college dorm.

I stopped hanging out with the people I had once considered "friends" because they felt too stuffy. My roommate Chi had recently moved to Arkansas when he graduated, and he'd probably been the only one that I would have felt okay to be around.

I was no longer 'Daphne Leblanc's prodigious artist son.'

I was less without her, and therefore I wanted less. Maybe a part of me even thought I *deserved* less. Things were difficult without her, but I was muddling my way through it.

My senior portfolio project for my Advanced Color Applications though?

Yeah, that was not happening.

Painting wasn't happening.

I'd found it nearly impossible to put a brush on the canvas since she– left. Hence the reason my project was still nothing but a blank canvas.

Dammit!

I needed to be able to do this.

Not just because I took pride in my grades, but because if I wasn't a painter anymore… well, I wasn't quite sure what I would be then.

Oh! Maybe some fresh air would help.

When was the last time I got some fresh air anyways?

I stood up and stretched the kinks out of my neck. I actually didn't know how long I sat there, *not* painting.

Thankfully my roommate, that had moved in at the beginning of the summer, seemed to have an allergy to his own bed, or he would think I had a few screws loose.

Meh, maybe I did.

I snagged my jacket as I exited my room, and made my way out of the dorms. It would get hot today, but this early in the morning, there was still a bite in the air.

There were very few people milling about the campus too. Not just because of the time of day, or the fact that it was a Sunday, but also because most students would wait until later today to get themselves back to campus and ready for classes tomorrow.

Well, except the freshmen.

They'd all swarmed in on Friday, and the rush of bodies had me hiding away in my room for most of the day.

I blinked slowly at the sign in front of me of a scarlet and eggshell white gryphon drinking coffee.

I wasn't sure when I decided to stop for coffee, but I shrugged and pushed open the door, sending the chimes above jingling to announce my arrival.

There was only one customer right now: an older guy sitting at the window, reading a newspaper. I didn't even realize they still made printed newspapers. He was probably a professor. The intellectual types always did seem to have more appreciation for physical copies of periodicals and books.

I walked up to the counter and ordered a cafe latte with honey. It was my go-to way to have coffee, and my mouth started watering a little in anticipation.

I turned around, not really paying attention thanks to the inner struggle over whether or not I should also order one of those cranberry muffins, when I smashed right into a gorgeous woman with a wild mane of black curly hair and two huge–er… eyes?

Ok, nope.

Tits.

Knockers.

Bazoongas.

Her boobs were big, and I was afraid those perky nipples would stab right into me.

"Oh geez, I am so sorry." I said, grabbing her arm as she stumbled backward a little. "Are you okay?"

She laughed, and it almost had the hint of a purr. "Yeah, I'm fine. I guess I was just focused on other things. Thank you for not letting me fall." Her voice oozed sex, and her tone said she could have made a killing in a career as a phone sex operator. "I'm Amy," she cooed up at me.

"Grayson!" the nasally sound of the barista called out to me, but 'big-boobs' snagged my arm and stopped me from leaving her.

"Would you? Would you maybe want to join me?" she asked, biting her bottom lip.

So sexy.

She was super sexy.

But just like so many other things from my old life, she didn't fit.

"Oh, I'm sorry. I'm taking mine to go. I have an appointment I have to make. Maybe some other time?" I tried to be nice and polite, but by the time I finished talking, she was almost wearing a sneer.

Weird.

I turned and grabbed my coffee, thanking the barista and wishing 'big boobs' a nice day. That almost-sneer didn't leave her face once, and suddenly I had this deep urge to get anywhere not here… really fast.

7

PRESCILLA BENNETT

I lined up the colored pencils on the work table before me and sat up straighter on the stool.

I wasn't usually so OCD, but I was nervous.

So nervous.

And I really had no reason to be. It was just class.

Something I'd done thousands of times over the years.

Sure, it was my first college class, but it was still just a class.

Right?

A curvy woman dressed in flowy layers of black gauze glided into the room. She was so graceful that my mouth fell open a little. Her wild hair curled all over the place in a natural afro that made me jealous for a second.

Then I tried to imagine combing it out and shuddered.

I'd stick to my braids, thank you very much.

While she had very dark eyes, her skin was a light mocha. She looked vaguely Mediterranean. When she glanced around the classroom to see who all was here, her eyes paused on me for a moment.

I swallowed and looked down. The urge to avert my gaze from her was fierce.

It was too much.

She was too much.

What was wrong with me?

I wasn't usually attracted to women. And I couldn't say that this was an attraction… exactly.

More like a desperate need to have her eat me alive. And that certainly wasn't like me.

I stared at my hands in my lap. They were clenching and unclenching without my conscious thought.

Geez, if this is what day one was like, I wasn't sure how I'd get through the fall semester.

"My name is Amy Gamal. Welcome to Intro to Art. The most important thing you need to know for my class is that there is beauty… in the chaos," she smirked. "As long as it's balanced properly. So let's begin."

Damn.

She wasn't just a student like I'd hoped. Maybe then I could have arranged to sit where she wasn't in my line of sight most days.

But she was my teacher!

A shiver ran down my spine as my instincts screamed at me.

Unfortunately, I couldn't understand exactly *what* it was that my instincts were screaming.

As Ms. Gamal began to lecture us on balance, I kept rolling the colored pencils back and forth under my hand. I tried not to look at her, but every time I glanced up from my fidgeting, my eyes would immediately land on her and catch.

It was like they didn't want to be anywhere else.

Even if that's not what my brain wanted.

After what seemed like months, the lecture came to an end as Ms. Gamal gave us instructions for which supplies to bring for the rest of the week.

I quickly packed up my things and tried to slide out of the room unnoticed.

I didn't know why, I just knew that I didn't want to catch her attention any more than I already had.

"Are you Miss Bennett?" her smooth alto voice questioned from behind me.

I froze halfway out the door, swallowed, and slowly turned back. "Yes, ma'am."

"Don't ma'am me," she said with a sexy smile.

Why was I thinking her smile was sexy?

"I heard you were new to town. Just wanted to welcome you to Polyville, Prescilla."

I blinked slowly at her. "Um, thank you, ma'am." I murmured. "I mean, uh, not ma'am. Um. Thank you."

There were thousands of new students on campus. Surely I didn't require a personal welcome.

I glanced toward the door, ready to just get out of here. But before I could move in that direction, Ms. Gamal reached up and pulled a little less than gently on one of my braids. "I look forward to getting to know you, *Prescilla*," she murmured.

Another shiver ran down my spine, and my stomach threatened to heave.

I nodded mutely and turned to run.

I had no idea what had just happened.

I had no idea why my body was responding to her like that.

But I did know… that I should probably look into switching art classes.

8

JACKSON MILLER

I walked along one of the many campus paths on my way to my next class.

Business Communications.

Like that was somehow different from regular Comm, which I already took–and aced I might add. But it was required, so here I was on my way to it.

Why the hell was Business Comm required for Music majors?

It didn't make any sense to me.

As the sea of students parted naturally around me, I let my mind wander over Scilla. At least, I think that's what her mom had called her.

She was so freaking gorgeous. Smooth skin that was rich as milk chocolate. Plump lips. Braids that I wanted to twist around my fist and hold onto while I licked the long column of her neck.

I needed to stop thinking about her.

Cary and I had some of the best sex of our lives the last couple of nights.

I knew we'd both been thinking about her. About having her between us. About bending her to our will; to Cary's. About what it would be like to kneel at his feet beside her.

And… there goes my cock! Ready to play.

Down, boy.

It's time for class. Not fucking.

As I approached the language arts building, I saw the door slam open and Jonathan storm out.

For half a heartbeat, I considered trying to hide so that I wouldn't have to talk to my irritating twin. But I knew it wouldn't work.

I could already feel myself being drawn to him. It had been like that our whole lives. Part of the burden of being twins. 'Twin-tuition' maybe?

Whatever it was, I continued walking his way. Hoping this wouldn't end in another one of his typical ego-driven blow-ups.

I'd had enough of it.

Enough of *him*, if I were being honest with myself.

Jonathan's head snapped up, and his eyes met mine.

He scowled at me, then intentionally turned on his heel and stomped off in another direction.

I slowly let out a breath I hadn't realized I'd been holding. That… went better than I could have expected.

I pulled open the door and headed toward the stairs.

This class was on the third floor, so I knew I could get a good stair climb in. However my climb was immediately halted when I looked up and saw the object of all of my naughty thoughts lately.

Now *this* was a distraction I wouldn't mind being a little late to class for.

We hadn't actually spoken yet, but I wasn't one to waste such a fine opportunity.

"Hey, neighbor," I said as a huge grin spread across my face. I was just so happy to see her. "What are you doing here?"

She looked down at me with a small smile. "Hey, you." Then her eyes widened like she'd just remembered something. "We haven't precisely met yet. I'm Prescilla Bennett." As she came down to the same step as me, she stuck her hand out for me to shake.

With a smirk, I took her hand and turned it to kiss the back, inciting a small blush as the coloring of her cheekbones deepened ever so slightly. "I'm Jackson Miller. But you can call me Jack."

"Oh, I can, can I?" Her laugh was like wind chimes. The soothing kind that tinkles quietly when a breeze blows through. *Not* the annoying clanky ones. "And your look-a-like that was leerin' at my mom the other day?"

I swallowed. "Please tell me Jonathan didn't say anything rude to your mom."

"I won't lie to you," she said softly. "She did say that he was carrying a few boxes and such. Did he move out?"

"Yes," I nodded, but her look of confusion had me quickly switching to a head shake. "I'd had enough. Funny how even identical twins can be totally polar opposites. Different in every way possible… except looks." I sighed. "But our new roommate is a gentleman."

The smile that crossed my face was genuine. I truly did enjoy having Meemo as our new roommate..

"He's very… arresting," she chose her words carefully.

I grinned even wider. "Yes, he certainly does draw people in. You should come by some time and meet him and Cary."

"I just might do that," she smiled. "Well, Jack, I'll see you around. I've got to get to my Western Civ class."

That's when I realized I still had her hand in mine. I kissed it again before I let her go. "I look forward to seeing more of you, Scilla."

"More of me…" She laughed again and continued down the stairs. "Oh, and only my mom gets to call me 'Scilla'! Later, neighbor!" she said with a wink.

There was no way the smile on my face was going away any time soon.

Less than five minutes with the woman, and she had me wrapped around her finger.

I pulled out my phone and shot off a text to Cary.

Her name is Prescilla Bennett.

CARY

You saw her? You TALKED to her?!

Yes. And her eyes are even more gorgeous up close. Her laugh...

I waited for another message to come through as I continued to my class. Surprisingly enough, I had actually made it here on time.

Strange.

It felt like I spent hours with her on that stairwell.

I was just sitting at a desk when his reply finally came.

CARY

You will not touch yourself today. No matter how tempting. You are all mine tonight.

Well, damn.

The man had spoken. No private breaks for me today.

I could not *wait* to get home.

9

CARY CARPENTER

I slipped my phone into my pocket and smiled to myself. That should have Jack nice and revved up for tonight.

But I also considered what he'd said.

Jackson had mentioned her eyes and her laugh. Not her silky skin or round ass or biteable lips.

No, he'd talked about her eyes and her laugh.

A sliver of jealousy wound through me. I wanted to hear her laugh. But then I chuckled at myself and my own stupid jealousy. What I really wanted was to see her laughing as she straddled my cock while Jackson took her from behind. Laughing… and moaning.

Begging.

Yes, that's what I really wanted.

I looked up in time to see Grayson, one of my classmates from last semester, walking across the street from me with his head hanging low.

Back then, Jack and I had lunch with Grayson a few times since our class had gotten out right at noon. He'd been really chill to hang out with.

Right now, he looked about a decade older than the last time I'd seen him. Which was a shame because he was one of the sexiest men I'd ever met.

I quickly looked both ways, then ran across the road to walk beside him.

"Hey, man," I said as I bumped shoulders with him. "How've you been? How was your summer?"

He stopped, turned, and just stared at me for a moment. Then he swallowed thickly. "I…" He swallowed again; it looked like he was choking on air.

Then he shook his head and continued trudging forward, only a bit slower than he had been a moment ago.

"Whoa," I said, pulling him to a stop. "Where are you headed?"

No answer.

"Can you skip your next class? You obviously need to talk." Something was very wrong.

He shook his head again, but stopped trying to walk away.

He stared down at the sidewalk while pain flitted across his face. Then it settled in to stay.

"Talk to me," I whispered, leaning close and trying to peer into his eyes. I was all up in his space, but he didn't pull away.

He just… stood there.

"She…" He swallowed thickly again. This time I saw the tears threatening to break loose. "She died."

Oh, fuck.

I didn't need to ask. I knew who he meant.

It could only be his mother, the most important woman in his life. I used to think my mom and I had a great relationship until I'd seen Grayson with his mom at dinner one evening. They were more than best friends. It was like they both were incomplete without the other. And not in a creepy Oedipal sort of way. In an unconditional love sort of way.

I admit watching them had made me a little jealous.

At least until Jackson had reached over and squeezed my thigh under the table.

Now I swallowed right along with Grayson and pulled him into my arms. Even though we didn't really have the kind of bro-hug relationship that I would normally expect before hugging someone.

"I'm so sorry, man," I said as I held him.

He slowly began to shake, letting pain out through his tremors.

"Come on. Let me buy you a coffee, and you can tell me all about it."

He didn't resist when I turned him and gently led him toward the coffee shop in the student union.

Once I had him settled in a booth with a cafe latte, I looked him in the eyes again.

"Alright, tell me what happened."

"It was breast cancer." He stopped for a minute and inhaled deeply. "It took her faster than I could blink," he whispered as he stared out the window at nothing. "She didn't even try to fight it... The life drained out of her almost instantly. And then she just... gave up."

"Oh, Gray," I said, reaching across the table to stroke the back of his hand. "I'm sorry. I know that had to be hard on you. Did you have help with funeral arrangements and such? Taking care of her estate?"

He gave a little sideways shrug, but otherwise didn't respond.

"What can I help with?" I asked. "Do you need me and Jack to come help you pack up? Need someone to go through donation items?"

Still nothing.

I let my gaze wander across him. He looked so much thinner than last semester. "Have you eaten at all since she passed?"

A small smile twitched at the corners of his mouth. "No... all that's done. The only things I have are in my room." He snorted softly. "Chi moved to Arkansas. My old roommate." He paused and shook his head. "The new one is never around, so I've got the room to myself..."

"And... eating?"

He hesitated, finally turning to meet my eyes. "I have eaten.

43

But… basically only enough to survive." He took a breath. "I haven't wanted to eat for… so long. Not wanted… anything."

I nodded in understanding. "Grief is like that."

I'd been super close to my grandfather before I'd lost him my senior year of high school.

I considered Grayson for a moment then pulled out my phone and started a group text with Jackson and Meemo.

> What do you think about a fourth roommate? He's got a dorm room, but I think he needs us.

MEEMO

> ::shrug emoji:: It's your house.

JACK

> As long as it's not my idiot brother, I'm good. A third is always welcome in our bed.

MEEMO

> Eww. No.

JACK

> I wasn't talking about you, Meemo.

MEEMO

> Wait! Aren't I good enough for your bed?

> Yes, you'd look sexy in our bed. We just didn't think you'd want to be there.

MEEMO

> Oh. Right. Good.

I laughed then looked back up at Grayson. He hadn't moved; he just sat staring.

"Would you… Do you think it might help if you're around people more? People who won't pressure you? Just… be there. Ready to listen when you need an ear or a shoulder?"

Tears pooled in Grayson's eyes again. "Maybe. I don't know… I really don't want to be around people right now."

"I understand," I said softly. "Jackson and I could use another roommate. We'll give you a good deal. But most importantly, we'll be there on the dark days."

"I'll think about it," he said with a sigh. "But not right now."

"Alright," I nodded as I patted his hand again. "Even if you don't move in with us, we'll be here for you. Come hang with us whenever your own thoughts get to be too loud. Whenever you need someone to help you forget."

The corner of his mouth twitched again. "As long as helping me forget does not involve your bed. You know I'm not wired that way."

My head fell back as I laughed. "Nah, man. That's not what I meant. You know it."

Okay, maybe it was what I meant.

A bit.

"I know," he said with a soft smile. "I know."

10

PRESCILLA BENNETT

*C*ollege was…

Well honestly, it's much like I expected it to be.

I'd only made it through my first week of classes, but so far it was all just like high school.

Except a lot more frat-bros hollering "Go gryphons" in the hallways. Oh and a lot more nudity later in the evenings around campus. And much more intense assignments.

Nothing I couldn't handle, though. I was actually a little relieved at the constant barrage of assignments. It kept me focused on my school work instead of the three yummy men next door.

I knew they were young, and probably close to my age. With the proximity to the university, you would think I would have guessed they would be students here.

Yeah, no.

It was still a complete tongue-tying shock to my nether region when I ran into any of them on campus.

Needless to say, I thought I was going to have to invest in some new toys. The panties just weren't going to cut it anymore.

I let out a small sigh at the thought, as I walked into my last class of the day. I tried *not* to make a sour face as I took my seat, but I was not at all excited to be here.

Not that I had any issues with art. In fact, it was usually my favorite class.

My issue lay solely with the professor. Granted, I had only had one encounter with her, but it was still really… terribly… uncomfortable.

Dropping the class would be a serious problem, though.

I was still undeclared in my major, which was fine except I kept leaning more and more towards something creative. That would absolutely make this class a prerequisite for any artistic field I chose.

It would also probably mean more classes with Professor Amy Gamal. Especially since I found out when I went to transfer to a different class that she ran the *entire* art department. And all of the Intro to Art sections were taught by her personally.

Yes, *all* of them.

Almost as if I summoned her with my thoughts, the professor walked into the room. The hair on my arms stood up, and I fought a shiver as her intense gaze met mine.

I didn't mind putting in the hard work for my grades, but I was starting to wonder if Ms. Gamal had more than just artistic techniques in mind for my schooling lessons.

"Hello, class. Today we are going to dive into something deep. You are welcome to use any type of medium you prefer, but I want to see one of your passions translated into a piece. There are no restrictions here, so make it as neat or messy as you prefer."

Passions?

Ok. I could do this.

What was I passionate about?

Oh… food!

Wait… was that weird? Could someone be passionate about food and not have any interest in cooking?

Well, I was just going to go for it.

What could I say? I loved a good cupcake.

I must have gotten lost in my work, because I lost track of time completely.

When Ms. Gamal warned us that there was only fifteen minutes left in class, I nearly jumped. I tried not to let the panic sink in, but time crunches always did that to me. I finished the cupcake with a few minutes to spare and decided to use them to clean up. Except when I grabbed my paint brushes, I accidentally smeared a huge streak of red right through the middle of the canvas.

Right through my pretty pink cupcake.

"Dammit," I whispered.

"Such a beautiful cupcake," a sultry voice purred in my ear. "Passions relating to our sense of taste are very profound since most of us are not fervent about something we require for survival. But I believe that anything involving our mouths is very passionate and incredibly *erotic*." Her last word was nearly a whisper, and I could feel her body almost pressed against my back.

Never in my life had I been attracted to another woman, and while a large part of me wanted to run away from her and drop this class, a tiny part of me fought the urge to lean back.

Why would I want to do that?

I glanced around and realized that all of my classmates had left.

Oh no!

This was the last thing I wanted. To be *alone* with her.

I took a deep breath and steadied myself. "Excuse me, ma'am. I need to clean my brushes and hurry to my tutoring session."

It was a lie.

School had only just started, there was no way I would need a tutor already.

I really hoped she didn't call me out on it, though.

I turned around, my face only inches from hers, and she stepped back a little.

Strangely, a small sneer flitted quickly across her face.

"I told you *not* to call me ma'am." She barked quietly at me.

I quickly moved around her and to the sink.

I hurriedly rinsed out my brushes and wrapped them in a paper towel. I would give them a proper cleaning when I got home.

When I turned around to grab my things, Ms. Gamal was blocking my way. I foolishly assumed she wanted an apology for the whole 'ma'am' thing, but I should have just left.

"I'm sorry Ms. Gamal. I—"

"Please, call me Amy."

"Yes, of course. Amy." It was impossible to miss the way she preened when I said her name. Or the way her nipples became impossibly hard and visible under her shirt.

And *why* was I staring at her nipples?!

"I do so *love* your accent, Prescilla. Perhaps we can get to know each other better *outside* of the classroom? It's nearly dinner time. I know how—" she trailed her finger up my neck and then gently ran it across my bottom lip, "*passionate* you are about food."

She moved closer, and her still hardened nipples rubbed against my arm. "Let me feed you."

Her last statement sounded almost like a command. A piece of me whimpered inside, maybe secretly hoping that she would just grab hold of me and devour—

Devour?

No…

That word made my stomach sour, and I stepped back from my professor quickly.

"I'm sorry, Ms. Gamal. I do need to get home." I awkwardly stepped around her and snatched my bag, not bothering to put my supplies away.

When I reached the doorway, I took a deep breath. I had to make a stand. Even a small one.

I didn't turn around, but I tried to project a confidence in my voice that I didn't really feel. "I am here to learn. I am here for class. Nothing more."

I had barely gotten the words out before my feet were moving under me. I didn't know if she said anything else, and frankly, I didn't really care.

I made a quick exit and found myself across campus in record time.

When I spotted the campus library to my right, I breathed a sigh of relief.

While I didn't have a tutoring session, there were a few books I needed to pick up.

It seemed like now was as good of a time as any.

11

GRAYSON LEBLANC

I had been walking around on autopilot all day.

So when a blur of a figure moving quickly away from the side entrance to one of the campus buildings caught my attention, I had to blink a few times before I could fully register what I was seeing.

Prescilla.

I knew she was attending PolyTech, and it made sense that she would be here with classes under way… but I still managed to forget.

Dammit.

I was such a shit friend.

I definitely should have gotten in touch with her sooner.

The truth was, I had been avoiding her. Well, thinking of her at least.

We had been friends since she was in middle school back in Louisiana. I'd been a sophomore in high school and her next door neighbor. When I'd decided to move to Polyville for school, my mom had come with me.

And I'd just… stopped talking to everyone back home. Not Prescilla. She and I had managed to text each other almost daily after I'd moved here. We spoke on the phone at least once a month.

Except, once Mom had died, I'd stopped calling or texting. I'd had to notify everyone back in New Orleans about Mom's death, of course.

I'd seen Prescilla briefly at the funeral. She hadn't been close to Mom, but she still had the look of hurt in her eyes when she saw me. Hurt that was a minor reflection of my own.

But if I were being completely honest with myself, that's not why I had been avoiding her either.

Somewhere in her transition from lanky, awkward pre-teen to delicately curvy woman, I'd fallen hard. It almost seemed to happen overnight. One minute I saw her as a little sister. Then suddenly, I was dying to know if her lips would taste like the apple lip gloss she favored. And the honeyed smell of her was enough to drive me wild.

So I did what I had since the moment I stepped in front of those freshman assholes that liked to pick on her. I protected her.

From *me*.

From my wild thoughts.

From the chance I would lose control and make a move.

From the chance of ruining our friendship.

From my need to check in with her nearly daily since I couldn't bring myself to hit "send" on any texts since Mom had died.

My brain finally pulled out of its little trip down memory lane, and realized I was on the move. Prescilla was moving fast, but I was faster. I caught up to her right at the bottom of the library steps.

"Hey, stranger! Where's the fire?"

She snapped her eyes in my direction, and a radiant smile plastered across her gorgeous face.

"Grayson!" She gave no warning before launching herself into my arms. Thankfully, they were empty, and I caught her easily, giving her a little twirl before hugging her close.

With her arms wrapped around me, it became immediately

apparent that Cary may have been on to something when he'd gently indicated I had lost some weight. I felt boney against her luscious frame, and not in a fun way.

Quickly placing her down before those thoughts dove deeper into dirtiness, I met her smile with one of my own. I hadn't thought I would smile like this again.

Prescilla was always the one person who could make me feel so... warm.

"It's so good to see you, Grayson. Sorry I didn't try to catch up with you sooner. I've been a little hyper-focused with school starting."

I chuckled at that. She had always been a little hyper-focused about school in general.

"It's okay. I should have reached out too. I guess I just haven't been—"

My thoughts cut off, and I suddenly couldn't find the words. How could I stand here and admit that I had been feeling like a part of me died, when this girl—no, this woman—could bring me to life in an instant?

She must have sensed the direction of my thoughts because she dialed down her smile, and it was filled with more sadness than I would ever like to see on her beautiful face.

"Oh, Grayson," she pulled me in for another hug, only this time it was gentle, and she rubbed her hands up and down my spine in a comforting gesture.

"You don't have to apologize for anything. You're healing. You're entitled to some distance." She pulled back then, and I felt colder with the sudden space between us.

"Thanks," I said lamely. Feeling awkward and eager to move the conversation forward, I latched on to the vision of her booking it across the green.

"So, what had you in such a hurry to get to the library? I don't think the books are going anywhere." I chuckled, but it was more at my dorky self than at my attempt to make a joke.

Ugh... Why was I so lame?

Thankfully, she stroked my bruised ego with a small laugh, but her smile didn't sit quite right.

"I'm just dealing with someone who is obviously not used to hearing the word 'no'. I think they get it now, but I was just eager to put some distance between us, you know? And I have some research I want to get a head start on."

My blood roared in my ears.

Someone was *hitting* on her?

She continued to talk, but I couldn't hear her over the murderous plot rampaging through my brain.

I had to find this guy and tell him to stay away from my girl, or else…

Wait.

She wasn't my girl.

My rage cooled off as quickly as it had built up.

I had no right to warn anyone away when I was too chicken to make any moves myself.

Her phone pinged, and she checked it, drawing my attention back to our conversation.

"Oh crap. I'm sorry, Grayson. I need to grab that book and get home to help with dinner." She turned to walk up the steps, but I snagged her hand for a second, causing her to stop and look at me again.

"Hey, you make sure to let me know if you need any help with that guy."

She scrunched her face up for a minute, but she smoothed her features quickly. "Thanks for that, Grayson, but I think I managed to get through to them this time. It shouldn't be an issue any more."

I nodded, and she turned to bolt up the steps.

At the top she turned back to me.

"Hey, Grayson. You should plan to come by soon for dinner. You're welcome any night. I think I sent you the new address, but I'll text it again just to be sure. The moms miss you too."

She smiled, and I nodded in agreement.

When she turned and disappeared behind the big campus library doors, my body physically deflated.

I suddenly felt very heavy again.

How could the woman who had always been my best friend twist me up in so many new ways?

Maybe I should make a move.

Looking down at my dwindling frame, I decided it was probably best to focus on pulling myself out of this rut first.

Maybe I needed to build some muscle back. Shave. The memory of Prescilla checking me out when we were swimming the last summer that I lived in Louisiana had me smiling. It even put a little pep in my step.

The way her eyes raked down my body and filled with desire, then embarrassment when she got caught, was a vision that was ingrained in my memory.

Yep.

Definitely needed to take a beat and get myself back on the right track.

The slight breeze changed directions, and I got a whiff of something foul.

Start with a shower, Gray.

Or several.

When *was* the last time I took one?

12

GUILLERMO PÉREZ

*O*k. I've got this.

I could speak English.

I could write English.

It may not be my first language, but I had adapted well and not been confused or felt like there was ever a language barrier for me. And no one had ever said anything about my accent being too thick to understand or anything.

So why did this damn text always read as a foreign language to me?

I'd already put off taking this English Composition class for two years and got some of my other courses done.

I was a junior class honors student… in a class full of sophomores.

Why was this shit so impossibly hard for me?

Half of the rules made sense, but the other half all seemed to contradict one another. And don't even get me started on the stupid fucking acronyms the professors teach… and then add 'special exceptions' to. That shit was *not* helpful at all.

Give me any rock in the world, and I could tell you at *least* five facts about it including the scientific name and density.

But English Composition?

Fuck, I hated it so much!

Well, that wasn't really true. I just hated that it took me so much concentration to actually catch on. I was normally able to comprehend my studies so easily.

This semester was going to suck balls.

This semester—wait, what day was it?

Oh right; it was Friday. I came to the library right after my last physics class. I wasn't sure how long I had actually been here. I knew it'd been several hours, since my eyes were starting to feel itchy.

I should probably head back to the house for some food and sleep.

I sighed to myself.

I was so glad I left home—and more importantly, farm work—behind so that I could do something more with my life and not spend ungodly hours toiling over the land.

I did not want to become like my older brothers. They were content with running the family farm.

If you looked too close though? They all seemed a little less than content with their fate.

I had to get away from that.

I wanted to actually *live* my life.

So what was I doing now?

Living in my text books.

I took a deep breath and reminded myself that this was just a temporary inconvenience to get me closer to my goals.

I had already battled my way to the top of my class. I would not disappoint the scholarship board by slacking now.

The smell of honey and apples filled my senses, and I bit back the groan trying to escape my lips.

My cock jumped to full mast, and I nearly dropped my head to the desk.

This had been happening a lot. Far more often than I would ever admit.

It was *her*.

Granted, it wasn't *actually* her. It was just the memory of her scent.

The smell that invaded my senses nearly every night. Flowing lazily from her bedroom window straight to my cock. That delicious all encompassing scent that almost managed to pull a deep rumbling purr from somewhere hidden inside me.

"I think you have spent more time scowling at that book in the past few minutes, than you have actually reading it. Maybe it's time for a break there, handsome."

The voice made me jump and hit my knees on the table. I dropped the book, and my gaze met hers. Standing so close and yet so far away. Her natural beauty took my breath away. Dark velvety skin and dozens of soft braids. I wanted to touch it all.

And her eyes. Those deep pools of creamy chocolate.

My gaze dropped to her lips, glistening as her tongue quickly swiped across it.

I must have had the strength of the gods on my side to remain glued to my seat, instead of throwing myself on her like I so desperately craved to.

"Are you actually here?"

Wait, wait, wait…

Did I just ask that out loud?

Why did I say that?

And why was my voice so high-pitched?

Her gentle laugh was enough to soothe my nerves almost instantly.

"Well, handsome, last time I checked, I was standing in the library trying to find a book for a research project. So I guess what I am saying is, I think so?" She paused for a minute and just stared at me. "Are *you* actually here?"

I didn't need a mirror to know that the stupidest grin I could ever have was plastered on my face. I sincerely hoped that she didn't think I was as stupid as I looked right now.

"I'm really here too. Although, I guess I should probably get heading back home soon. It's nice to know I am not imagining you this time, though."

Oh *fuck*!

Why was my brain so hell bent on making me act like a complete fucking idiot in front of the girl I was pining over?

Somehow, I managed to keep my expression calm. Even though internally… I was screaming.

"So, you've been imagining me, huh? Well it's nice to know I'm not the only one." The smirk dropped from her face as horror washed over it with the words she'd just admitted.

Nice to know I wasn't the only one that couldn't seem to wrangle control over the words that seem to just fly right out of their lips.

I covered my mouth to stifle the laughter that tried to break free.

While our quiet conversation had been ignored, I didn't think that such a boisterous sound would be welcomed.

We *were* in a library after all.

"Well now that I have managed to make an ass out of myself, I have to get going. I'm sure we will see each other a lot." Her eyes widened at her words. "I mean like really seeing each other, not just fantasizing. Oh shit. Okay, I am going to leave before I keep saying stuff I don't want to say out loud."

She gave an awkward little wave, as she moved quickly towards the exit.

I had an overwhelming urge to chase after her.

Chase.

The thought had my blood roaring in my veins and excitement pooling deep inside me.

If it weren't for the raging boner that was impossible to hide right now, I probably would have.

I shook my head and moved to slowly start putting away my stuff.

I had everything in my bag except the English Composition book.

I attempted to scowl at it and the knowledge it was trying to keep from me. But then I realized that I had a new appreciation for Comp.

After all, if I hadn't been scowling at this damn book, would she have said anything to me today?

So yeah. Maybe I kinda liked English Composition a little bit now. It was my icebreaker with–

Fucking hell!

I never even got her name.

I sighed and scrubbed my hands down my face.

It was fine.

This would not be our last interaction.

Not with the way my body was reacting to her.

No, this was only the start of our dance.

I smirked a little when I thought back on our conversation.

So she had been fantasizing about me.

That deep purr nearly rose to the surface again, and I had to tamp down the sound.

And of course… my dick was stiff all over again.

I was going to be stuck in this library until it closed if I couldn't find a way to get rid of this damn boner.

13

PRESCILLA BENNETT

I turned on my heels and fled out the main doors of the library.

And promptly ran into a wall of man-chest.

Geez!

This is why I shouldn't do two things at once.

I looked up and right into startlingly deep brown eyes.

Oh, my…

"Well, hello, beautiful lady," the rich voice crooned. "Jack tells me your name is Prescilla?"

Jack?

Who was– Oh!

The non-sleazebag biker twin neighbor with the soft hands.

"Yes," I couldn't help but smile. "But he failed to tell me your name."

He gasped dramatically and gripped his chest. "He failed to mention that his boyfriend– the devilishly handsome man that practically lives to worship at his feet– is named… Cary?"

"Cary?" I asked.

I'd vaguely remembered him saying that name. But I'd be

lying if I said a little part of me wasn't disappointed to find out that they were gay. And together.

Why were all the sexiest men gay or taken?

I mean, I had suspected as much after that scorching kiss they shared, but I was sad to have it confirmed.

"Like… Cary Grant?"

"Exactly!" He grinned from ear to ear. "You are the first person ever to get that right on the first try."

"Wait. Really?" He had to be joking. "Why else would you be named Cary?"

"It's what my mom saddled me with," he shrugged before his smile turned into a sly grin. "So… are you a classic movie fan, Prescilla?"

"Very much so." Astaire had been my favorite, but I thoroughly understood why everyone loved Grant, too.

"Maybe we should have a classic movie marathon sometime soon." Was it my imagination, or had Cary stepped closer to me?

He pitched his voice a little lower, and shivers of desire ran down my spine. "Make a comfy pillow pile in the living room. Some fresh popcorn. Dim lights. Jack sprawled out, looking so pretty."

My breath caught in my throat as his spicy scent washed over me.

Damn.

"That sounds perfect," I squeaked.

I must have been crazy!

I didn't need to put myself in that kind of environment with a guy whose boyfriend was a really great guy. That was just asking for trouble! Even if the boyfriend were there…

Wait.

Was he suggesting… both of them?

Had I understood him correctly?

But maybe that's exactly what I needed though.

To stop thinking about Ms. Gamal. To move past the pleasure-pain of seeing my old friend Grayson, but knowing that he'd lost his mom and I hadn't really been there for him. To settle this nervous embarrassment left over from talking to Mr. Smexy. God, I needed help.

"How does tomorrow afternoon sound?" Cary asked. "We'll order in pizza. Spend all Saturday curled up. Getting our golden age Hollywood on."

"It's a date," I squeaked again.

What was up with the squeaking?

"Perfect," Cary cooed again.

Yes, he was definitely closer to me now. When I looked up into his eyes, they seemed more black than before. Almost like the chocolate brown had just had a bottle of black ink dumped into it.

Swirling brown and black.

Mesmerizing.

I leaned closer to him. I couldn't help myself. I sucked in a deep breath of that spicy scent. "See you tomorrow," I whispered.

Then… I ran away.

Because my panties were inexplicably soaked. And if I'd stayed any longer, he might have ripped them off me.

And if I'm being honest with myself here… I don't think I would have even tried to stop him.

14

JACKSON MILLER

I dropped my messenger bag onto my desk and toed off my shoes.

If I was going to have a full load this semester, I really needed to consider pausing the band for a while.

Who knew junior year of music composition would be so exhausting?

Tonight's "Welcome Back to PTU" show had gone well. But like all gigs in the smoky clubs downtown, it took all of my available energy and then some.

Why was it so much harder to play until two in the morning when school was in session than when we were on break?

But I wasn't sure I wanted to make the call to pause us.

Not yet.

We made the best gig money during school, after all.

Cary had been having dinner with his parents tonight, and I suspected not having him in the crowd was part of the reason tonight's concert had worn me out so much.

My man gave me energy.

Which was odd considering how many people I'd heard

complain that his personality just sucked the life right out of them. They just didn't understand him.

Overall, today had been a long week.

I was so ready to do nothing this weekend. Granted, I *couldn't* do "nothing" because I had a ton of work due on Monday that needed my attention.

God, I hated homework.

I fell onto my bed and stretched out, tempted to sleep, but knowing I needed to get up and see about food. I wasn't entirely sure when the last time I'd eaten was.

Before I could get up, though, my bedroom door swung open, and my man walked through it.

Instantly, my mouth began to water, and my dick filled. The stress of the day melted away like an ice cream scoop dropped onto concrete on a hot summer day.

A new, buzzing energy began to fill me just from *looking* at Cary.

"Hey, sexy. You're looking especially fine tonight. Are you here to eat me up?"

A glint appeared in Cary's eyes, and a smirk slid up his face. "Funny you should mention that. I did have something very much like that in mind."

Oooh…

A shiver ran up my spine, and I very carefully held still, rather than running into his arms like I wanted to. He hadn't told me to get up yet. Though, he hadn't told me to stay either. Knowing my Dom, he wanted me laid out exactly as I was.

So I stayed.

And stayed.

And tried real fucking hard not to fidget.

And kept still while he just stared at me… undressing me with his eyes.

"How was the concert tonight?" he asked.

"Fine," I sighed and gave up on the expectation that we'd be having sex in the next few minutes, letting my body relax again. "They piped too much fog into the room. And the light board had some kind of technical glitch that had them flashing a half beat off from our music." I looked up at the ceiling before slowly closing my eyes. I was just so tired. "It was exhausting. I think you're my good luck charm because I always have more energy when you're there."

"Funny. I was just thinking that being at a Bloody Gorgeous concert always fills me with energy." When I slid open an eye, he smirked at me. "Did you meet Kris's new girlfriend yet?"

"Oh, Cary," I grinned up at him. "She's this petite little thing, with these big puppy dog eyes, who absolutely adores my Kris."

"We'll have to have your little sister bring her by for dinner one night."

I laughed. "She's not my little sister," I protested. "But you're right. I'll set a date with her for them to come over."

"Good." He nodded.

His eyes roamed my body.

Finally, he took a single step into my room and kicked the door closed behind him. "Shirt off," he said in that sexy, gravelly tone he always had when he was really turned on.

I immediately sat up and pulled my t-shirt over my head. I flung it in the general direction of my hamper, though I knew Cary would make me pay for the lazy messiness later.

Well… Maybe I did it *because* I knew Cary would make me pay…

"Unzip your jeans, but do not pull yourself out yet," he commanded.

I decided to torture both of us a bit, so I unbuttoned and unzipped my tight jeans as slowly as humanly possible. The whole time, I kept my eyes locked on Cary's face.

I licked my lips just thinking about having him.

Sucking his beautiful cock down my throat.

Kissing along his angled jaw.

Feeling his balls slap my ass as he pounded into me.

Once my jeans were fully unzipped, I dropped my hand to the bed next to my thigh.

No touching.

One of my least favorite rules ever was Cary's favorite.

Come to think of it, it was likely his favorite *because* it was the one I struggled with the most. Once my hands were both back on the blanket and I was stretched out before him, Cary's eyes twinkled, and he stepped forward between my knees.

"I have been craving you all day," Cary growled. "I ran into Prescilla at the library, and all I could think about was her. Between the two of us. Writhing in pleasure. Unable to control the lust coursing through her veins. And you, on the other side of her, showing our girl just how sexy she truly is."

I swallowed the longing that shot through me at the vision he conjured.

I needed that.

Him.

Her.

All of us together.

So very, very much. "Th–that sounds like fun."

Cary threw back his head and laughed.

It went straight to my rigid cock.

Damn, I loved his laugh. "Good. Because it's happening tomorrow."

"Wh–what?" I choked on some saliva that had pooled in my mouth just from watching my man laugh.

"I invited her over for a classic movie marathon and pizza tomorrow afternoon."

"Oh," I sagged a little. That… wasn't quite what my mind was picturing. Or what my cock jumped for joy at the thought of. Still…

"And based on how her reaction was very similar to yours just now, I'm fairly certain sex will be on the table as well." Cary's sexy smirk grew a bit more. "Now lose the jeans."

"Yes, sir," I swallowed again and quickly moved to comply.

15

CARY CARPENTER

*J*ack laid there in just a tiny pair of briefs with a raging hard on.

He was truly beautiful, and damn, I loved every inch of him.

I knelt on the bed, straddling his hips, and leaned over to lick the artwork across his chest.

He had a mandala flower made of ancient symbols that covered nearly the entire right side. And all of that expanse of black ink just begged for me to try a taste.

It really didn't matter that I'd run my tongue over the designs hundreds of times before. I wanted to do so every day for the rest of my life.

His skin held a hint of salt; he'd probably sweated up a storm under the stage lights tonight.

I wish I'd been there to watch him perform. It didn't matter what the venue or the style of music, he was always grace personified, music come to life, the sexiest one on the stage.

And I'd missed it tonight.

Damn.

Not that I regretted dinner with my parents, but I really loved Bloody Gorgeous gigs.

Jack groaned, arching into me. "Best. Investment. Ever," he gasped out.

"Hmm?" I was having a hard time processing what he was saying because my fingertips had found his nipple on the left side and were pinching and pulling it.

"The tattoo is the best investment I've ever made," he whispered. It was so breathy that it made my cock swell against his where I was sitting on him.

Then what he'd said caught up to me.

I sat up and grinned at him. "What can I say? It's delicious."

He forced out a laugh, but I noticed his knuckles turning white as he gripped the blanket on either side of him. He was being so good trying not to move.

I debated for a second ending his torture.

But then, that would end my delight.

I leaned back down to pay his other nipple proper tongue homage, then slowly licked down his ladder of abs. That is until his cock bumped up against my chin.

Time to go lick somewhere else.

I slowly made my way up his oblique and to his pecs.

God, I loved every inch of my man, but his muscular torso with that intriguing ink was definitely my favorite.

I licked.

I bit.

I nibbled.

I sucked.

I hummed.

And I tortured us both by slowly aligning our cocks, but only barely letting them touch.

When I found my mouth on Jackson's carotid, felt his life's blood beating against my tongue, I lowered my body so that all of my weight was on his. I wanted so badly to bite down on his neck, but I just held my lips open, breathing him in.

And I just.

Held.

Still.

It wasn't long before the shaking began.

First it was just Jack's hands trying to keep the blanket in his grip. Then his forearms and biceps trembled. Then his back was arching, and his thighs were quivering along either side of mine.

Once he began to open his mouth to protest, I finally moved again.

I leaned up to capture his lips in mine and bit down hard on the bottom one. At the same time, I thrust our cocks together. I gripped his hips and ground into him. The taste of copper filled my mouth as Jack's lip bled, and I nearly went insane with lust.

Lust for my man.

Lust for Prescilla.

Lust to have the two of them together.

After a few thrusts, I knew Jack was more than ready to come, and I certainly was. "Come now," I growled. And he did.

After several minutes of his juices soaking his little briefs and the front of my jeans, he stilled.

"Goddamn you," he whispered. "I thought you were going to bite me."

I leaned up so that I could watch his face as I smirked at him. "Oh, we're just getting started. Biting will happen tonight." And I couldn't wait to be bitten.

He moaned the delicious moan of a man that'd been sexually tortured and satisfied.

But the night was only beginning.

16
PRESCILLA BENNETT

I sat up in bed, covered in sweat and panting.

What in the *hell* was I dreaming about?

I couldn't remember, but my damp clothes, hardened nipples, and throbbing clit made the context of the dream obvious.

Heat prickled across my skin in nearly visible waves.

Okay, I clearly needed some fresh air.

I pulled myself out of bed and tried to ignore the tingling sensation when I walked. It was nearly enough to make me come undone.

What the hell?

Orgasm by walking?

That'd be a new one.

I pulled the curtains open, quickly unlatched the window, forced it open, and embraced the cool breeze that welcomed me.

After a few steady breaths from the colder night air, I felt... well about halfway relaxed. But, I would take that as a win.

Feeling much calmer, I let my eyes drift around the backyard.

Momma's inherited flower garden beds still looked lovely, even though the weather was getting a little colder. Some of the flowers would start to hibernate here soon. It would be sad to lose a little of the color back here, but I was sure that Momma had a plan for that. She seemed to always have a plan for everything.

I was looking all around the yard, not really focused on anything in particular, when something grabbed my attention. I must have seen a shadow shift or a light flicker somewhere, because my gaze was instantly pulled to the most gorgeous pair of eyes I have ever seen.

And the hunk in the neighbor's yard that owned them was looking right at me.

He was stretched out in one of the lounge chairs with a book open on his lap. His shirt was mysteriously gone, so his wide chest was on display. He only had shorts on. Wasn't he chilly? After a second or two, I realized that I was staring, and that he could clearly see me.

A brief wave of panic rushed over me, and it was then that my brain flatlined, and my body decided that waving like a total creep was the right course of action.

Why did it seem like this guy always managed to make me do awkward things? It wasn't his fault, of course.

Why the hell was I still waving?

Thankfully I managed to stop my flailing limb, and my super hunky neighbor waved back.

Oh wait a second, I think he was waving me down to him?

Well, who was I to deny a sexy *almost* stranger in the middle of the night?

I gave him the finger—no, not *that* finger. You know, the "hold on a second" finger.

I got so excited that in my quiet rush down the stairs, I forgot that my pajamas were quite thin. Like, you could probably see my nipples thin.

I debated a little about running back up to change, but I worried that he might be gone if I took too long, so I snagged my new PTU Gryphons hoodie from the coat peg where I'd left it earlier, and tossed it on.

Better than nothing, I supposed.

I stepped out the back door and made my way over to the side gate. Hunky neighbor was already waiting for me.

I couldn't help but smile at him. His face was just so... I mean there was really nothing about this guy that wouldn't be labeled as a hunk.

"Hello," His deep voice vibrated my spine and sent a jolt straight to my–

"Oh fuckkkkk!"

My eyes went wide, and I stared at the house and the direction of the voice belonging to someone who was *clearly* enjoying themselves tonight.

When I looked back at my late-night friend, he was covering his face with his hands. Clearly he was not amused with his enthusiastic roommates.

Oh my–

Roommates!

That meant the voices were Cary and Jackson.

The thought of the two of them going at it–well, I hadn't known I was into that sort of thing, but my nipples hardened to sensitive peaks, and I bit the inside of my cheek to keep me grounded.

"Sorry about the–uh, noise."

And just when I thought he couldn't get any hunkier, he blushed.

I shrugged. "It's alright. At least someone has a reason for being up late tonight."

He chuckled at my dorkiness.

"So I take it the noise is what encouraged you to enjoy some fresh air tonight?"

Why was I so lame?

He pursed his lips like there was something he wanted to say, but he just nodded at me instead.

He didn't say anything as I walked further away from the gate to the cozy chairs near the pool and flopped into one.

Since I didn't want to just stand around, and going back to bed held no interest right now, I had decided joining him was best.

"Have you settled into the new house?" he asked softly.

"I like it. It has a bit more space than the old one. Plus the neighbors are pretty cool. Even if I don't know his name." I winked at him and hoped it came off as flirty and not like I had something stuck in my eye.

He face-palmed. "Shit, I'm so sorry." He turned and faced me before thrusting his hand in my direction. "Guillermo Pérez, but my friends just call me Meemo."

"Meemo. I like it! Mine's Prescilla Bennet. I don't have a cool nickname. Unless you count what my dad called me when I was little."

"Okay, now my interest is piqued. What did he call you?"

He smiled with his eyes, and it felt like I could get lost in them.

He still held my hand, even though we'd stopped shaking a bit ago. His hand was huge and nearly engulfed mine completely. But his grip was gentle and the skin soft and… why was I analyzing his hand?

I realized that he'd patiently waited for me to answer, and a blush covered my cheeks.

"He used to call me PB."

He laughed a little. "Like your initials?"

I laughed too.

"Not exactly. I mean, it is my initials, but I used to have an addiction to peanut butter." As the words left my mouth, I realized how his skin was almost that same creamy shade. I wondered if he tasted like peanut butter.

His husky voice startled me, but it was heavily laced with lust. "Why? Would you like to find out?" Why did that sound like an invitation?

My eyes nearly popped out of my head.

He laughed at my reaction. "You may have mumbled a few thoughts out loud."

Damn my sleep-deprived brain.

"Sorry about that."

"Don't be. But I do wonder, do you still have a peanut butter addiction?"

There was no mistaking it this time. It was definitely an invitation.

I looked at his lips and didn't let myself hesitate any longer. I would blame it on the lack of sleep in the morning instead of the overwhelming pull I felt toward this man.

My lips were on his in an instant.

His free hand twisted into my braids and brushed gently across my scalp. The sensation caused me to moan, and he took the opportunity to tilt his head and deepen the kiss. I ran my tongue along his bottom lip, and he growled hungrily.

Soon our tongues were engaged in a feverish dance. Each vied for control over the other.

When his teeth nipped my bottom lip, a single idea boomed into my brain.

Mine.

And it was that word that had me breathlessly pulling back.

He looked just as shocked as I did. Like he'd heard my thought.

Come on, PB. Get your shit together.

You can't go around kissing strangers and then claiming them as yours.

17

GUILLERMO PÉREZ

We sat there, silently staring into each other's eyes, trying to catch our breath.

This was not my first kiss, but damn if it didn't feel like it.

My heart was racing a mile a minute and my brain was buzzing.

She blushed and stood, still holding my hand in hers. When she started to pull away, I kept my grip on her hand and finally stood. Moved a little closer.

Her gaze shifted down to our hands, and her brow creased slightly.

"What was that?" She asked me in a quiet, breathless tone.

Did she mean the kiss? The heat between us? The obvious attraction we shared? Or did she feel the same pull to me that I was feeling to her?

Before my brain could catch up to formulate a response, she started talking again.

The confusion was gone from her face, and a warm smile had replaced it.

"Thanks for the company tonight, Meemo. I should get back

to bed. I have our weekly family breakfast in a few hours, and it's my turn to cook."

I reluctantly let go of her hand and stuffed mine in the pockets of my shorts.

When she dropped her hand to her side, it caused the unzipped hoodie she had on, to gape a little. Showing more of the thin cotton pajamas she had on.

And the incredibly hard nipple trying to poke through.

I quickly averted my eyes and held in a groan.

Fuck, she has got to be the sexiest woman alive.

After a few breaths, she started to turn. I did the only sauve thing I knew…

I waved like a fool and said, "Nighty night, PB."

She snickered a little before disappearing back through the gate and into the house.

I let my head fall back and just looked up at the stars for a minute. They were beautiful, but even now they just felt so– muted. When compared to the sexy woman I just made an ass of myself in front of at least.

What the hell, Meemo?

"Nighty night"?

Was I going to warn her against imaginary bugs in her bed next?

That kiss had my thoughts in a complete jumble.

Bugs in her bed? Really? It was none of my business *what* was in her bed.

I glanced up at her window and saw the light flick off.

Of course, that didn't mean I would be okay with anyone else finding out what was in her bed either.

That thought had me growling low in my chest.

I shook my head. I had to get myself together. Maybe I just needed a good run to clear my mind.

I stretched and warmed my muscles up a little before I took off down the trail behind the house. I was so happy to find out that the guys' rental property included this big portion of woods back here. And the deer trails made for easy run paths.

After only ten minutes, my mind started shifting back to Prescilla.

That kiss was amazing. The thought that came with it, though, had been a bit intense. That deep in my bones feeling that she was *mine*.

The only way she could be mine was if *she* wanted that. I couldn't just declare something like that in my mind and suddenly it was so. Maybe I should give her a little space? Let her come to me?

Yeah, that's what I'd do.

I came to a complete stop when I remembered that she would be at the house later today.

A 'movie night' was what Cary had said. Although the conversation had gotten incredibly short once he'd realized that Jackson was home.

And then the sounds quickly followed the closed door.

I wondered if Prescilla sounded like that? She probably sounded even sexier.

My cock twitched again, and I fought the urge to punch it.

Logically, I knew that would hurt. But damn, I was so sick of sporting a constant stiffy.

Resigned, I told myself that I would give Prescilla some space.

Just maybe *after* the movie night, because there was no way in hell I would miss that opportunity.

I had no clue what movie they were all planning on, but hopefully it wasn't some cheesy RomCom.

18

GRAYSON LEBLANC

I caught a glimpse of myself in the shop windows as I walked by.

It hadn't even been a full twenty-four hours since I pulled my head out of my ass, but I could already see the improvements in my reflection.

Cleaner. *Obviously*.

But also in my posture.

In my eyes.

Both showed more confidence than I had felt in days.

Hell, more than I had felt in *months*.

I couldn't keep living in that dark bubble. I was ready to actually start *living* again.

And damn, did that realization feel nice!

I managed to get a nice meal in me last night after my shower. I even did a little sketching. Granted, they were all different angles of a certain angelic face, but still.

Sketching was progress.

I didn't sleep all that great, hence the trek to get some super strong coffee, but I didn't cringe away from my easel when I woke up this morning either.

That was also progress.

What was that stupid cheesy saying again? All progress is good progress?

I had no damn clue, but I did know that while I didn't feel completely healed, I did feel *better*. And that was something I was incredibly grateful for.

As I neared the coffee house door, the delicious smells inside wafted out to greet me. My stomach grumbled in appreciation of the aromas as well.

Hmm… I had a banana, but there wasn't a rule against a chocolate croissant with my coffee. And I did need to be a little more generous with my calories.

I opened the coffee shop door, and as I stepped in, my stomach grumbled louder at the cacophony of sounds and even stronger scents that slammed into me.

Maybe I should get a blueberry muffin too.

Distracted by my growing order, I slammed right into the person in front of me.

The apology nearly rolled off my tongue, but stopped short when she turned around.

It was 'big-boobs.' I mean, Ms. Gamal. And boy did she have the girls on full display today.

You would think being a professor would make her more keen on modesty. But I honestly didn't think that word was in her dictionary.

Granted, she wasn't like any other professor I'd ever known.

When she had walked into the studio and began her lecture the first day of class, I nearly fell off my stool. A new teacher for my senior year?

And then I began hearing the whispered rumors…

How Mrs. Cornish, the awesome head of the art department had suddenly disappeared, and Ms. Gamal had taken her place.

How Mr. Fraley, who I'd had for five semesters, had transferred to some university out West.

How other art teachers seemed to be gone.

Just… gone.

I had compared notes with other art majors and found that nearly everyone had her for all of their art classes. If not all, then most.

Just how many classes was she teaching?

And how many students was she blatantly coming onto like she had been me this past week?

Snapping my gaze back to her face and away from her half-exposed breasts, I found her winking at me.

It took all of my strength not to visibly cringe, even though I totally did on the inside.

"Hey there, stud," she purred at me.

She reached out to touch the buttons on my shirt, but I quickly backed up and took her hand in mine. Turning it into a handshake. The move didn't go unnoticed by her, but she only quirked an eyebrow at me.

"Hello, Ms. Gamal. Sorry I ran into you. I was so focused on coffee and breakfast, I wasn't really paying attention to anything else." I added a smile that I hoped looked polite.

"It's no problem at all, Gray. And please, call me Amy."

"Actually it's *Grayson*, Ms. Gamal."

She shrugged a shoulder at me in response and finally let go of my hand.

"You know, I find myself quite famished this morning. Maybe you would like to join me somewhere that will let us better satiate our appetites?"

Her innuendo and implications were so thick, I nearly gagged. I couldn't believe I found her even remotely arousing before. Granted, it'd been before she'd ever opened her mouth. But still…

"Next!"

Saved by the barista again.

"I think it's your turn, Ms. Gamal."

"I'm afraid I won't be able to get what I really want to devour from the barista."

Was she really that thick?

Could she not see that I tried to politely brush her off?

I actually didn't even know what to say anymore. I mean, she *was* the head of the art department, so I didn't think telling her to "fuck off" would go over well for me graduating next semester.

So instead, I let my stomach, which now grumbled louder, do the work for me.

"Oh, I'm sorry to hear that. If it's okay with you, I'm going to go ahead and order." I didn't even give her a chance to respond. I maneuvered around her and placed my order for a honey latte with two extra espresso shots, a chocolate croissant, a blueberry muffin, *and* a cheese danish.

Why?

Because I was hungry, and now I was also stress-eating.

Better than not eating. Right?

Right!

With my order placed, I moved around the counter and was already being greeted by pastries.

I spared a quick glance to the spot where Ms. Gamal still stood and nearly peed my pants.

No one in line had moved around her, probably too afraid to get too close.

The anger rolled off her in palpable waves. Her death stare sent ice through my veins, and her sneer turned the face I once thought attractive into a nearly monstrous expression.

I didn't know how long I stood there. Frozen in fear.

The barista snapped his fingers, and I was able to drag my attention away from the woman with that murderous gleam in her eyes. He handed me my drink and the last of my pastries.

I debated my options for how to leave the coffee shop, but when I turned towards the door, Ms. Gamal was gone.

I had a bad feeling in the pit of my stomach that pissing her off had been a grave offense.

Good thing I had yummy pastries to bury that bad feeling deep.

Very, very deep.

19

AMY GAMAL

I saw red. Nothing but red.
Surrounded in it.

Covered in it.

Devoured by it.

But that's not how this worked.

I was the one who devoured.

The thought that I let petty emotions dictate my actions right now, made me even angrier.

How dare he?

He should grovel at my feet. Beg for a mere touch of my perfect skin. Moan for a single taste of my body.

Instead, that bastard was drowning himself in pastries.

I hoped he got fat on them. That would be a fitting punishm–

My thoughts became laser focused and the predatorial sneer that crossed my face was enough to make the people on the side-walk give me a wide berth. Some even quickly jay-walked across the street to avoid me.

Good. They should fear me.

Grayson LeBlanc had insulted my advances for the last time.

He could have been a delicious little pet.

Now he would be the bug under my shoe.

I ran my fingers lovingly across the hood of my 1958 Plymouth Fury. I had this baby painted red as a tribute to my favorite human novel. At least they had good horror stories.

Books and this car were the only human guilty pleasures I had.

Thankfully, my baby was an incredibly sturdy weapon, and the cherry red finish would work in my favor nicely. Just like it had from time to time, since the day I'd bought it straight off the line.

Now I just needed the right opportunity.

I laughed deeply as I crawled into the driver's seat.

Yes, this institution was the perfect choice.

Let the chaos commence.

20

PRESCILLA BENNETT

I shifted on my feet as I knocked on the door.

I'd been looking forward to this all morning.

A chance to get to know my neighbors better. A chance to watch movies I loved. A chance to eat as much pizza as I wanted! A chance to cuddle between two sexy men. And if the cuddling led to more, I certainly wouldn't complain.

The door swung open, and Cary stood there, grinning at me like I'd brought his favorite dessert.

I hadn't.

I hadn't brought anything because he'd insisted.

I'd asked if I could bring a pie or a bag of popcorn or even just money for pizza, but he'd just kept shaking his head.

So. Here I was without a gift for my host.

And yet he was still looking me up and down like I was something delicious.

"Hi," I managed to squeak out. "Am I too early?"

"Not at all," Cary smiled and reached out to take my hand. Pulling me into the foyer. "You could have come at two this morning and it wouldn't have been too early."

I blushed because that was about the time that Meemo and I

had been in the backyard. There's no way I would have interrupted them.

I squirmed a bit, trying not to think about it too much. My special panties had already gone through two sets of batteries this week. I had a hard time looking Cary in the eye when I'd been thinking about him… *them* so much.

"So what are we watching first?" I asked as I turned into their living room.

I stopped in the doorway and gawked. They'd pushed all of the furniture to the edges of the room and the center had been piled with loads of pillows and cushions. Blankets covered them all, making a huge nest.

It looked absolutely perfect.

Jackson looked up from his spot on the pile and smiled at me. "Hello, beautiful! How about we start with *White Christmas*? The cooler weather has me wishing for snow right about now."

"Oh, I love Danny Kaye!" I exclaimed. "I mean, he's not Fred Astaire, but he'll do." I winked at Jackson as I settled onto a cushion near him.

Not too near him. Not all up in his business or anything.

But definitely close enough to *accidentally* brush up against him.

"Oh, that's how it is," Cary laughed as he sat down next to me. Considerably closer than I'd sat beside Jack.

There was no accidental brushing against me. His side was pressed against mine, our thighs aligned. I did my best to hold in a shiver of desire. It was nearly as bad as when I'd been with Meemo early this morning.

My face heated again as the thoughts of Jackson and Cary in bed together assaulted me.

"We have *Funny Face* for sure. And some more of his," Jackson said as he scooted closer to me, pressing against my other side.

Suddenly the image that Cary had put in my head of Jack laid out all pretty came back to me.

I licked my lips, but wasn't sure what to say.

"I brought snacks!" Meemo called as he came in the door from the kitchen. He smiled at me and handed me a big bowl of popcorn. "What are we watching first?" I smiled up at him as Jackson stood to put in the movie. Meemo sat down next to me and scooted close.

"Hey!" Jackson said when he saw. "That's my spot! I want to sit next to Prescilla."

"Oh, sorry. I thought you wanted to sit by your boyfriend." Meemo shrugged.

"After last night, I think Jack has had enough of me!" Cary laughed.

"Never." A noise between a playful laugh and a hungry growl came from Jackson as he sent a smirk Cary's way.

Damn, they were hot.

"Thank you for the popcorn," I whispered to Meemo.

He blushed a little, but nodded at me.

God, that blush of his was going to kill me!

It made me want to crawl into his lap and kiss him until neither of us could breathe anymore.

To claim him as *mine*.

And there it was again.

Mine.

I desperately wanted to kiss him again. And again. And again. Every day for forever.

But I didn't think I could make that kind of claim after knowing him less than a week.

Well, really less than a day that I'd known his name.

"I have a speech on Monday," I blurted out. Awkwardly.

Because apparently that's who I was now. Awkward, lame PB.

"Why we have to give our first speeches after three classes, I have no idea." I continued to ramble on lamely. "But I'm nervous as fuck because… speaking. In front of… people." I didn't have to force the shudder in response to the vision that flashed in my mind.

I truly did *hate* talking in front of people.

Meemo nodded vigorously. "It's horrible to stand in front of people and prove that I know what I'm talking about."

"Yes!" I hissed. "Just let me write a paper and be done with it."

Cary looked between the two of us, his mouth hanging open. "You hate speaking in front of people?"

"Don't you?" Meemo and I asked at the same time.

"Nooooo…" Cary shook his head slowly. "I'd rather give a speech than write a paper any day."

"I'd rather you all stop talking so that we can watch Rosemary Clooney," Jackson said as he settled down next to Cary, leaning into his shoulder.

We all laughed but then settled into the nest.

This was shaping up to be the best afternoon I'd had in a long time.

21

JACKSON MILLER

Meemo volunteered to walk Prescilla home.

All twenty feet between our front doors.

But Cary and I just waved goodbye to them and then headed straight to my room.

"Did you see the way he looked at her?" Cary asked as he closed my bedroom door and slipped his hands around my waist.

"Yes," I nodded. "He is so far gone for her."

"I've never seen him like that," Cary mused. "He's pretty much ignored everyone around him the whole time I've known him. I always had to force myself into his space to get him to talk to me. But he just… opened up and talked to her like they'd been best friends for years."

"Or lovers," I noted as I pulled Cary even closer to me.

"Or lovers," Cary agreed. "I think that's it. I think he wants her so badly that he's forcing himself past any fear because he just wants to be with her."

"Should we…" I paused, unsure how to phrase my thought.

"Back off and let him make his move?" Cary asked.

"Yeah," I nodded. "I mean, she's gorgeous and funny, and I

definitely want her in our lives. But if she's the one that Meemo will come out of his shell for, I think we should encourage that."

Cary nodded before nuzzling his face into my neck. "Sounds good," he whispered.

"It was so fascinating observing them, wasn't it?" I asked. "I felt like some kind of weird zoo visitor. 'Here we have the male homo sapien courting the female in all his dorky glory. Note the female's response.'"

Cary laughed and cuddled closer into my chest. "I can't wait to watch episode two of 'Super Natural Love.'" He reached around to pinch my ass.

"Why are we still dressed?" I asked.

"Are we done talking about Meemo yet?"

I laughed. "We can be."

"The thing is," Cary looked up without pulling away from my chest. "I think Prescilla is ours. My gut says that she's perfect for us. That she's part of our family."

"I felt that from the very beginning." I ran my hand up Cary's spine, pressing him closer still. "I think that's why I got so mad at Jonathan for yelling at her."

"Note that we both feel she's more our family than your own twin," Cary hummed.

"Yeah," I laughed. "But he's a jackass so that's no loss on our part."

"But all that means is that I think we should wait until Meemo has established a relationship with her," Cary leaned in to kiss my collarbone.

I shuddered and thrust my hardening erection into his.

"Okay. We wait for Meemo to get his shit together. Then we make her ours." I nuzzled into the side of Cary's head. "Are we done talking about Meemo now?"

"We can be," Cary smirked up at me.

When I grinned back, his smirk quickly slid into his Dom face. "Strip."

"Yes, sir," I chuckled and jumped to obey.

22

CARY CARPENTER

I licked my lips as Jackson pulled his shirt over his head.

God, my man was so fucking sexy.

Solid muscle, intricate tattoo, dark hair and eyes, a dusting of hair across his chest.

But it wasn't just the way he looked. It was the way he moved. The way he spoke. His incredible brain. His passion for music. How full of life he was.

I felt incredibly lucky that we'd met at such a young age and that I'd known right away that Jackson was mine.

He sometimes complained about the fact that we had lived through our awkward junior high puberty stage together. That some couples had an advantage because they didn't have those painful memories of each other. But I disagreed.

All of those memories just made him even sexier today.

"Do you know what I spent all afternoon dreaming about?" I growled as I reached to unbutton Jack's jeans.

"Um, a PB sandwich?" Jack looked at me with uncertainty.

We'd noted that Meemo had called her 'PB' almost exclusively. And that every time he did, she blushed a little more.

It was definitely my new favorite name for her.

"No," I grinned. "A Jackson Miller sandwich. With Prescilla riding your cock and me railing you."

"Oh, god!" Jack moaned. "I thought we were going to step back for Meemo."

"Oh, we are," I smirked as I slipped my hand beneath his briefs and pulled him out. "But that's not going to stop me from fantasizing about having her and my man together."

"Please," Jack whimpered. His knees were trembling, barely holding him up. I released him to walk around behind him. I shed my shorts and shirt on the way to the bed, then turned to sit on the end of it.

"Kneel," I said with a low growl.

Jack spun around, then quickly moved to kneel between my thighs.

As he watched my cock fill, he swallowed heavily. "Please," he begged again.

I wrapped both of my hands around the back of his head and pulled him toward me. "Suck me off like the dirty boy you are," I commanded with a gentle tug.

A shiver ran down Jack's spine, and he quickly leaned forward to take me into his mouth. He reached up to grasp me, but then promptly put his hand back down when I tsked.

"This is what we're going to do, my love," I whispered as he bobbed up and down on my aching dick. "We're going to help Meemo win the girl. And have dirty, dirty sex every night. And once the two of them have no doubt they belong together, we're going to invite them to come play with us."

Jack nearly choked on the moan that rose from his chest at that image.

I smirked and rubbed one of my hands from the back of his head down his neck and spine.

"And once they both realize that they can't live without us, we'll make them ours." I gripped Jack's neck as he groaned around my cock. "Because whether they know it or not, they're already ours," I added as an afterthought.

I pulled Jack off of me and drew him up from his knees. He quickly straddled my lap, and I captured his lips in mine.

After being so close to Prescilla and Jack all day without getting to taste her, I was simply starving.

I licked and nipped at Jack's mouth. "So hungry," I moaned. "Need you now."

"Yes!" Jack cried out. Then he pulled away to nuzzle my neck. "Take me."

I flipped us over so that he was on his back.

"I love you," I whispered. Then I reached over to grab the lube.

As rough as Jack and I both liked it, we both also liked to be safe. I'd pounded him pretty hard last night, and I knew he was sore today. He'd done plenty of squirming on the cushions during the movies.

I smirked as I thought about the fact that his favorite position in our little nest today was his head in Prescilla's lap, on his side, with his ass pressed against my side and his legs tangled with mine. Prescilla played with his hair while I had easy access to the skin of his back. And his ass. Not that I'd played with it in front of Prescilla; it was still a bit early in our relationship with her to do that. But I'd been tempted by it all day.

I opened the lube and poured it all over Jack's dick, balls, and down into his crease. He tried to stifle another moan, but it broke free. I rubbed lube into his ass and then maneuvered my cock toward his entrance. As he reached up to tangle his fingers in my hair, I slowly pushed into him.

Home.

I was home.

In my man.

In our bed.

Wrapped around each other.

I didn't want to be anywhere else.

I massaged more lube over Jack's dick then began a slow rhythm.

After a full day cuddled up with Prescilla, we were both wound tight.

In the fastest orgasm either of us had had since that very first time we had sex at fourteen, we both came apart. I gasped as Jack covered us both in come and I filled him up.

Yes, this is where I wanted to spend the rest of my life.

Right here.

The only thing that could make it better was if Prescilla were with us too.

But maybe that wasn't what fate had in store for her.

"Love you," Jack whispered as he drifted off to sleep.

I'd certainly kept him from sleeping last night. Maybe I'll let him sleep some tonight.

I gently pulled away to grab a washcloth to wipe him up, but stopped short.

Nah, I'd wake him up again in a few hours to dirty him all over again.

I smirked at that thought.

I loved a dirty Jack.

Maybe I would get lucky at one point and have a dirty Prescilla too.

23

PRESCILLA BENNETT

I sat on our front porch, sipping coffee and listening to Mom and Momma joke about how I was too good for their hash brown frittata.

As if.

I loved the dish. When they added bacon to the top, it became my favorite breakfast ever.

But I was still so full from yesterday's movie marathon.

It almost felt like a "how much can we feed PB marathon" instead.

The guys had fed me popcorn then pizza. Then Meemo made empanadas, which were—oh my god, yum! Then Jack pulled out a gallon of triple chocolate fudge ice cream.

How could a girl say no to that?

Cary had kept my cup filled with sodas. Then tea and lemonade mixed. He brought me chips and seven layer dip. Jack made pancakes around midnight or so. Meemo pulled out a fresh fruit mix from thin air, as far as I could tell.

Yeah… I was still stuffed.

Just coffee would do this morning. I'd finish off the rest of the hashbrown frittatas for lunch.

In the meantime, I just smiled at my moms and enjoyed the porch swing and the cooler air.

I'd not been sitting there very long when I saw Meemo exit the house next door. He had a huge backpack on and looked like he was headed to campus to study.

Oh, yeah. I should probably practice my speech for tomorrow.

But instead of acting like a normal person and waving at him before heading inside to do my own homework, I jumped up to meet him at the edge of my yard… and tripped down the porch stairs.

Literally tripped.

"Hi," I might have sounded a little breathless, but it was because I nearly face-planted in front of him.

I mean, it couldn't be because just the thought of kissing him turned me on like crazy. "Are you headed to the library?"

Oh, geez!

What was I saying? Why was I asking the obvious?

I'd spent over an hour already this morning trying to talk myself *out* of asking Meemo out.

The feelings I kept having for him.

The thoughts and dreams?

They were all just so… intense.

But now that I had the chance to see how he felt, I was going to ask about school?

"Yeah, I've got a paper I want to start on," Meemo looked down at my feet and blushed a bit. It made me wonder what the paper was about.

"Wou-would you like to have dinner with me, once you're done?" I didn't sound like I was begging, did I? Hopefully. Please let me have sounded normal.

"Did you get enough sleep last night?" He glanced up at me and then back down. Why was he asking that? What did how I slept have to do with us going to dinner?

"Um, yeah," I nodded. "I woke up earlier than I would have liked, but I got enough."

"Oh," he nodded. "That's good."

"So, I'd really like to… have dinner with you," I said. "If that's too much, then maybe we could grab coffee some afternoon?"

"This paper I've got," Meemo said, looking up at the sky, "is about themes of friendship in Shakespeare's comedies. How all of the lovers are really just friends." He bit his lip and looked over my shoulder toward the porch.

I shifted my weight so that my face was in front of his and he had to look at me. "That sounds interesting."

"Oh, it definitely is," Meemo nodded and still managed to not look at me. "Anyway, I've got to get to it." Then he turned and practically ran down the street toward the university library.

Damn.

What had I done wrong?

I thought things went really well yesterday. By the end of the night, he'd been curled around me as we watched *Singing in the Rain*. Yes, I'd been nervous about asking Meemo out, but mainly because I'd never actually asked a guy out before.

I hadn't *actually* thought he'd turn me down.

That he would run like a crocodile was chasing him. Or a lion.

What the hell?

I turned back to the porch, confusion and worry eating a hole in my stomach.

Obviously I'd done something wrong; I just wasn't sure what.

The best way to deal with a rejection was with carbs. I'd learned that long, long ago.

I wandered into the kitchen and pulled down a plate to serve myself some hash brown frittata. I piled the cheesy, bacony goodness onto my plate until there was none left in the pan.

Hopefully Mom hadn't expected to have leftovers.

I carried the plate up to my room, replaying every single moment from yesterday through my mind.

Where had I gone wrong?

24

GUILLERMO PÉREZ

*T*here was only one logical conclusion.

I was a fucking idiot.

I knew that I had planned to put space between PB and me. But when she actually asked *me* out, I nearly lost my resolve. Instead, I went on a tangent about the campus library and the paper I was working on.

I mean, it wasn't a *lie*.

I really was headed to the library to work on this paper. It just wasn't due until next week, so I still had plenty of time. But that didn't change the fact that I'd blatantly rejected her.

And the look on her face?

I stopped myself from opening the door to the campus library. This was bullshit.

I was never going to get any work done today. Not when I kept thinking about how fucking deflated she looked.

That beautiful face was never meant to look like that.

I rubbed my hand down my face. *Fuck this.*

I turned around and headed back to the house.

Maybe I would get lucky, and she would still be sitting outside. Then I could just fix this whole thing and ask her to dinner.

Yeah, that's what I'd do.

But what about this constant pull toward her?

I didn't want to get into such a heavy relationship. There was no way she would be interested in that. Not so soon.

Dating? Hell yes.

This feeling that I was going to marry her and bind her to me forever? Uh, no.

But then, people my age usually slept together when they were dating. That brought up a whole other set of problems.

Could I really force myself to be a gentleman and take things slowly with her?

I thought back on the kiss we shared early yesterday morning. Even the more subdued one from last night when I walked her home.

No.

There was no way I could stop myself.

I wanted her.

I *craved* her.

I wondered if she felt the same? And would she even want me to take things slow?

I was still fighting with myself on whether asking her to dinner was a good idea or not when I got to our road.

A quick glance showed me that there was no one on the porch. When I looked around a bit as I walked past, I noticed the car wasn't in the driveway anymore either.

Damn.

I barely registered walking up the steps to the house or walking inside, but I had worked up some serious anger and took it out on the door when I closed it.

At the sound of the slamming door, Cary jolted up from the couch where he'd been sleeping.

"Sorry," I mumbled half-heartedly as I stomped to my room.

Was it childish? Yes.

Was this all my fault? Also yes.

I closed the door to my room with more care and thumped my head against it, letting my book bag drop to the ground.

This was bad.

This was so fucking bad.

Getting this upset about a missed opportunity with her? I was in deep.

My padré's poor advice rang in my head. '*Nunca te enamores demasiado de una mujer a menos que planees mantenerla.*' (Never fall too hard for a woman unless you plan to keep her.)

But maybe that was the real issue here.

Maybe I really did want to keep her?

25
CARY CARPENTER

I stared after Meemo as he walked to his room and closed the door more quietly than he had the front door, and I frowned.

Something was wrong. Something was *very* wrong.

I wondered what had happened.

Should I go talk to him?

Yes, I definitely should.

I stood, walked into the kitchen, opened up the fridge, and peered into it.

There didn't seem to be anything useful. Except maybe the leftover dip from yesterday. I grabbed it. When I opened the pantry to grab some chips, my eyes landed on a bottle of red wine. That would do.

I put together a little tray of snacks and walked down the hall toward Meemo's room. I knocked gently and leaned my head onto the door jam. "Meemo, I've got some food. And something to drink."

After nearly a minute of silence, right when I was about to knock again, Meemo swung open the door.

He looked absolutely wrecked.

He just stood there, staring at the tray in my hands, but not moving or talking.

"Tell me what happened," I said as I gently used the tray to nudge him into his room.

I followed him in and kicked the door closed with my foot. I set up the snacks on his nightstand, and crawled up onto his bed.

Why the hell was this bed so high?

Oh, wait. It was the bed Jonathan had and left behind when we kicked him out. Douchecanoe Jonathan probably wanted a high bed for fucking purposes.

"Sooooo?"

"She asked me out."

"Excellent!" I grinned. "So why don't you seem happy about that?"

"Because like a complete idiot, I turned her down. And then ran away." He sat on the bed next to me and began picking at a loose thread in the comforter. "Like a scaredy cat."

I snorted. "And why'd you do that?"

"I panicked," Meemo admitted. "My brain froze up thinking about forever with her, and then I couldn't focus on right now with her. And I just... *ran*."

"Forever?" I asked quietly. "You've known her less than a week and you're thinking about forever?"

"She's..." he paused and looked up at me, there was so much pain in his eyes. But also hope. "She's it for me, Cary. I'm never going to want anyone else but her. One kiss is all it took for me to know that."

Oh, wow.

This was much more serious than I thought it was.

This changed things. Something like this doesn't happen as often.

Without saying a word, I reached over and poured a glass of wine for Meemo.

I handed it to him then grabbed one for myself.

"That one kiss and she felt like... *mine*," Meemo whispered before he took a sip.

He sat staring off into space and didn't say anything else.

Ah, so he thought this was a pity party.

Fuck that!

"So, what are you going to do to win her?" I asked after a moment or two of silence. "You're not going to give up, are you?"

Meemo shrugged and took another swallow of wine. This time it was a much bigger gulp.

"No, you're not, man," I bumped my shoulder against his. "Faint hearts never won fair lady."

Meemo looked over at me like I'd lost my damn mind. Perhaps I had. "Why are you talking like that?"

"Robin Hood?" I asked.

When he stared blankly, I continued on. "It's a quote from the Robin Hood cartoon. You know, when he–oh fuck, never mind. The point is, if you're willing to do something about it, I'll help you win her back."

"I'm scared," Meemo whispered. "If she says she doesn't want a… someone like me, then I won't be able to recover."

"She won't reject you," I nudged him again. "Not when I've got your back, making sure she sees just how great you are."

When he slowly nodded before taking another large swallow of the wine, I couldn't help but grin. "Excellent! Time to plot and plan!"

Meemo rolled his eyes, but he also sat up a little straighter.

The hope in his eyes began to push past the painful despair.

He could do this.

If she truly was his one, he *had* to do this.

26

JACKSON MILLER

When I opened the door after an awkward dinner with my grandparents and Johnathan–the idiot hadn't bothered to tell them I'd kicked him out; he'd just moved into the dorms and given the school their bank account number!– the first thing I heard was… giggling?

What the hell?

Who was giggling?

Why were they giggling?

Wait… I knew that giggle.

That was… well, hell.

I threw my jacket on the kitchen counter where a bag of chips lay open.

Hmm…

Cary hated stale chips and didn't usually leave the bag unclipped.

I stalked down the hallway, wondering what the fuck was going on.

It wasn't that I would have minded if Cary brought home some extra entertainment for our bedroom tonight, and I absolutely trusted him. But that giggle. It had me choking down my jealousy.

I found them in Meemo's room. They were both sitting against the headboard, chips and glops of dip all over them… and the comforter.

A nearly empty bottle of wine sat on a tray.

Ah, yes. That made sense now. That was the giggle of a very *drunk* Cary.

I'd just never heard Meemo's drunk giggle before.

But I heard it clearly now. They were both squinting at me and giggling like I'd done the funniest thing on earth. They seemed more drunk than one bottle should have made them.

I wondered what they'd been talking about.

"How are the chips?" I asked cautiously. Cary's answer would give me a good idea just how drunk he was.

"So stale," he giggled. Again. "But nice and salty. Have you had this seven layer dip? You've got to try it, Jack."

"I had some yesterday," I pointed out. "When Prescilla was here?"

"Oh, right." Cary grinned. "I remember that."

Maybe he wasn't as far gone as I'd initially thought. The bottle wasn't empty yet, and surely they'd had about the same number of glasses.

And then I spied three more empty bottles on the floor next to the nightstand.

Oh boy…

"*Prescilla*," Meemo purred her name and then sighed heavily. "I'm going to marry that girl." He flopped over to his side and grinned up at me. "Isn't Prescilla such a beautiful name? But it's a bit stuffy for her though. I really like PB." Another giggle escaped him. "She wanted to know if I tasted like peanut butter."

I raised an eyebrow at him. "And did you?"

"I have no idea," he cackled. "We got distracted by…" He shook his head. "It was a great kiss," he concluded.

"So why are you two trying to get drunk?"

"Oh, we weren't," my boyfriend protested. "We were plotting the wooing of a fair lady!"

"Good god!" I shook my head, then pointed at them. "I get the rest of the wine. You two have hit your limit."

"No," Meemo frowned. "We didn't have that much. I only had one glass. Or maybe two? I probably stopped somewhere around three or four." Cary started giggling again. "But I'm going to win her over. Just you watch!"

"Oh, I believe you," I nodded as I grabbed the wine bottle. It was emptier than I'd first thought.

I took a long swig. When I pulled the bottle from my mouth and licked my lips, I caught Cary staring at my mouth. I smirked at him. "Meemo, are you done with my boyfriend?"

Meemo looked back and forth between me and Cary. "Uh, yeah. Leave the rest of the chips and dip, though. I'm still hungry."

"Of course you are," Cary smirked. But he quickly crawled off of Meemo's bed and followed me to my room.

It seemed he was eager to finish off the bottle of wine with me.

And I wasn't going to complain a bit.

27

PRESCILLA BENNETT

I was such an idiot.

I'd not been able to get Meemo out of my head since yesterday's car crash of an encounter. I knew there was always a chance that I'd be shot down. That someone wouldn't want to go out with me.

But I honestly thought Meemo wanted to. That he wanted me as much as I wanted him.

But, no.

He'd practically run away from me.

It hadn't been a car wreck. It'd been a train wreck. An oil spill in the ocean level disaster. My new 'Most Embarrassing Moment Of My Life'.

And that was saying something since the last one had been Grayson catching me ogling his swimsuit and…muscles years ago.

God!

Why was I so awkward?

Why did I always make a total fool of myself in front of the guys I liked?

It was the worst.

Wait, no. The worst was that I totally tanked my speech this afternoon because I couldn't get Meemo out of my head. I completely lost the thread of my presentation. I blanked out when there were questions at the end.

If I'd been coherent for more than ten seconds of it at a time, I'd be shocked.

It had been a disaster. One even bigger than an oil spill. We're talking hurricanes, earthquakes, tornados, volcanos, and tsunamis all hitting the same city at the same time.

I sniffed back the tears that had been threatening since yesterday.

This was ridiculous. I didn't recognize this weepy, distracted girl.

I hated her.

Time to pull my panties up and take my life back. Meemo would just miss out on all the awesomeness that was Prescila Bennett. Too bad for him.

Speaking of panties...

I pulled out my phone and quickly did a search. What I wanted was only four blocks away. God bless college towns!

I put my phone back in my bag and began walking, a smile finally spreading on my face.

I didn't need a man.

Any man.

Especially not a scared little boy like Meemo.

Okay, he wasn't that *little*, but he was still acting like a scaredy cat.

I was my own woman.

I would be successful and happy whether or not I was dating anyone.

Whether or not Meemo was mine forever.

I. Didn't. Need. Him.

I nodded firmly, reinforcing the idea in my brain, since I couldn't get my heart to even remotely listen to that train of thought, as I pulled open the door to the shop.

It was much dimmer than I had expected. There were just neon and black lights sporadically interspersed throughout the vast area. But each wall stood had a beautiful display of one specific type of item or another.

It took me less than two seconds to find the one I wanted.

The dildo wall.

Oh, yeah. Baby's First Dilly was coming home tonight!

I would have *all* the orgasms all by myself. And I wouldn't even be thinking about that silly boy at all.

Nope.

Not thinking about him.

Not even right now.

"May I help you?" a lady behind a counter asked.

"Yes," I turned toward her with a grin. "What's your longest-lasting dildo?"

She smiled and led me toward the wall, "This is definitely the one with the highest durability rating." She pulled down a box with a creamy tan dildo in it. It was huge, and the color and smooth texture had me thinking about peanut butter.

Peanut butter flavored kisses.

Peanut butter skin.

I wondered if Meemo's dick looked like–

Hell to the no.

"Any one but that one," I shook my head a little too enthusiastically.

I did not need a peanut butter dildo.

"Is there one that looks like jelly instead?"

28

JONATHAN MILLER

I was as hard as I could possibly be.

Yeah, I might have taken a viagra just for kicks.

I smacked Tina's ass hard as I pounded into her. Or maybe it was Nina?

I railed into her hard, and she cried out. Probably because the bitch was drier than the Sahara Desert.

Oh well. Not my problem.

I looked to my left and checked out my reflection in the full body mirror again.

If I were into weird shit like my brother was, I would so fuck me. I was one hot son-of-a-bitch.

Speaking of bitch…

I slapped Gina's ass again and nearly lost my load at how fucking hot I looked pounding into her.

"What the actual *fuck*, Jonathan? Are you just watching yourself in the mirror?!"

She pulled away from me with an audible pop and flew off the bed, snagging her clothes from the floor.

"Where the fuck are you going, Sabrina? Can't handle all this dick?" I grabbed myself and gave it a little twirl.

She spun around and narrowed her eyes at me. "First of all, sex with you is so fucking boring! I nearly fell asleep. Secondly, it's Katrina!"

She flung the door open and stalked down the hallway. Not even caring that she was naked in the guys' dorm. Probably going to try and find another dick to fall on.

What a ho.

I kicked the door closed and walked over to the mirror. I snagged the lube off my nightstand and squirted some into my hand. Running my slick hand up and down my shaft sent a shiver across my skin.

The viagra wasn't getting me where I wanted, so I used my free hand to pop an X into my mouth and wash it down with my second bottle of tequila.

Or was it my third?

I didn't know.

That bitch Lena drank like half the first bottle anyways.

I watched myself in the mirror again. No wonder pussy flocked to me. I looked like a fucking sex god.

I stroked myself fast and pinched my nipple hard.

Fuck that felt good.

I pumped harder as the pressure in my balls increased. The room started looking a little fuzzy, but I ignored it as I exploded all over the mirror. My legs shook, and I stepped back to flop on my bed.

Only I missed and landed hard on the floor.

Wow! That must have been some good X.

I didn't feel that at all.

I looked around my room and didn't even try to hide the sneer. This place was a fucking dump. It was still better than living in my asshole brother's house though. I wasn't allowed to have any drugs at all in there.

It was such bullshit. And he made me clean up after myself. And buy a new kitchen counter after he caught me fucking those twins on it. We didn't *mean* to crack the counter.

He was worse than Mom and Dad.

I didn't even care if "speaking ill about the dead" really was a thing.

They could rot.

Same with Jackson.

He'd been such a dick last night at dinner. Ratting out to our grandparents that I was using their retirement fund to pay for my room. Horrendous little room. Such an asshole.

They always say some bullshit about how twins are close and share some special bond. Complete bullshit. I have fucking hated his guts from the moment we were conceived.

I tried to kill his weak ass in the womb, too.

I tried to kill him a few times over the years. Mom always just said it was a phase and that I was just getting my frustrations out.

Stupid bitch.

I wanted that asshole dead.

After they died though, I kinda let that thought go. Afterall, he would always give me money and take care of shit for me.

Whatever.

Thinking about all this shit was killing my good mood.

I snagged the tequila and finished off the last of it. Letting the burn coat my throat all the way down.

I needed to get out of this fucking room. It was killing my buzz. And besides, I could probably score a much better looking pussy and pound out the rest of my irritation.

I got up—which took a lot more effort than it really should.

Why did it feel like I was so fucking heavy?

I swung the door open and a cool breeze wafted across my body.

I looked down and remembered that I was naked.

Oh shit, and still sported a serious stiffy. A *very nice* boner.

I snagged a pair of shorts, sans boxers, and shoved my feet into my flip-flops. It felt cooler outside, but I always ran hotter, so I would be fine.

I walked down the hallway and stumbled down the single

flight of steps that ended at the exterior door. I may have missed a step or two and smacked into the door, but I didn't give a fuck.

With Mina and my room behind me, I took off down the campus sidewalk.

Time to go prowling for pussy.

CARY CARPENTER

I chuckled as Jack told Meemo about dinner with his grandparents last night.

I mean, the two of us had always known what a giant dick Jonathan was, but Meemo was just finding out. And his outrage was hilarious.

"No, he didn't!" Meemo shouted, his hands over his face like he just couldn't bear to look.

"Yes," Jack nodded gravely. "The ass gave the school our grandparents' retirement fund account numbers. What does he think he's going to do when he's eaten through everything they've earned? He certainly won't be the one taking care of them! Douche."

"I've had my disagreements with my padré, but I can't imagine just stealing from him like that!" Meemo's outrage was cute.

"Okay, enough," I grinned at the two of them as I pulled the chicken cacciatore out of the oven. "Jonathan is now a banned subject for the rest of tonight. Eject him from your mind and tell me how wonderful dinner is."

Sure, I was laying it on a bit thick, but I did not want to talk about the jerk any more. And pretending to be just as much of a narcissist as Jonathan was a fun little game I sometimes played when Jack needed to lighten up.

"Oh, it is so wonderful!" Meemo immediately said. Maybe he'd caught onto my little diversionary tactic. "Definitely the best... uh... chicken... thing... ever."

"Chicken cacciatore," Jack laughed. "And it is seriously good. One of my favorite things Cary makes."

"Aww," I smirked at my boyfriend. "You're so sweet. But you don't have to lie like that. I'll still tie you up tonight if you ask nicely."

Meemo choked on the gulp of water he'd just taken a sip of. "I did not need to know that," he gasped out as Jack pounded him on the back. "Feel free to *never* give me those visuals ever again."

"Look how red his ears are, Cary," Jack laughed. "I think you embarrassed our sweet Meemo."

"You two are so weird," Meemo scowled at us. But then he started laughing. "You two *do* realize that these walls aren't thick enough to block out all the noise you make, right? I'm well aware of what you two get up to."

Jack immediately began blushing even redder than Meemo had been, but I just laughed.

"Welcome home, Meemo. Welcome home." I winked at him then began dishing up the food.

"Who taught you how to cook?" Meemo asked. "Mamá wouldn't let me into her kitchen. Even if she'd been on fire and I wanted to save her. Nope! '*No hay chicos en mi cocina!*'" He said the last bit in, what I can only assume was his best impression of his mother's voice, but it was truly absurd.

Jack and I laughed until my sides hurt.

After a few moments, I was able to get myself under control and answer him.

"Jack's grandmother, actually. When Jack's parents died, his grandparents took them in, and I would spend all my time over there. She's really fun to work with. And helping her in the kitchen meant that I got to eat the hot cookies right out of the oven and not wait for them to cool like Jack and Jonathan had to!"

"I knew there was a reason you were always helping her!" Jack cried as he playfully swatted my arm. "You just wanted all the hot cookies for yourself!"

"Always," I said with a grin. "I want *all* the cookies."

Meemo choked again. "You meant to make that sound dirty, didn't you?" he accused me.

"Always." I grinned even wider.

Jack threw up his hands in the air, but Meemo just laughed. It was definitely good to hear him laugh today. He'd been so down yesterday.

Granted, I think our guys' night in might have helped his mood a little.

It had definitely made my night better.

"So what are we doing after dinner tonight?" Jack asked. "I've got a composition I'm supposed to be working on. No band practice tonight, though. Thank god."

"I was thinking of going for a run," Meemo looked a little sheepish at the admission.

"Oh, definitely go run!" I encouraged him. "You spend too much time hunched over that table in the library. Go stretch your muscles."

"You say that like I don't run every damn morning!" The outrage was back in his voice, but this time it was obviously playful.

Good, he knew we were teasing him. Lovingly, of course.

"I'm going to work on that project for Applied Chemistry," I looked toward Jack.

"Great. Homework it is." He nodded. Then a little smirk slipped free. "And after homework?"

Meemo groaned. "And now I'm done with dinner!" he cried out with absolutely no conviction.

Jack and I both laughed.

30

GRAYSON LEBLANC

*T*he cooler air felt fantastic.

Especially after being holed up in my room for the past three hours straight.

A crowd decked out in red and white crossed the green shouting, "Go gryphons" and other such sporty chant encouragements.

I guess it must have been a game night? I'd missed the whole thing.

Not that I minded one bit. I wasn't a huge sports fan to begin with, but I had been busy tonight.

I looked down at the paint on my hands and smiled.

I did it! I actually broke through my wall and painted.

It might be a few days late. And it certainly wasn't a Van Gogh or anything. But the little field of sunflowers had been stuck on my mind, and when I started with the paintbrush, it just flew out of me.

Once I finished, it wouldn't be mine though. I painted it with someone else at the front of my mind. I just hoped she would love it.

I hoped that when I gave it to her, Prescilla would understand what I was trying to say. What I should have said years ago.

My stomach growled again.

Right!

Focus.

I needed food.

I spotted the neon lights to the ramen joint across from campus and couldn't stop from rubbing my hands together.

Yum.

As I continued walking down the path, something moving on the right caught my attention.

There was a half naked guy stumbling across the green.

What the actual fuck?

If it were a Friday night or Saturday night, I could totally understand a drunk student wandering around. It happened most of the time in fact. Even if it was a streaker with all the game partiers.

But stumbling around alone, on a Monday night?

And how was he *not* freezing?

He moaned loudly and stumbled in my direction.

I had a brief moment of panic and nearly yelled 'zombie!' when one of the path lights hit across his face and I was able to get a better look at him.

He looked like Cary's boyfriend Jackson. But his hair was different. I glanced down, and my eyes immediately shot back to his face.

Well the guy was walking around with a serious boner, and he was one lucky guy with how big of a weapon he was packing.

Not that I was interested in that kind of thing. It was just kind of hard to miss right now. Sticking out in front of him, altering his balance. Or lack thereof.

He moaned at me again. I looked up at the beautiful pink neon sign proclaiming "White Lily Ramen" and tried to suppress the whine.

My stomach grumbled again.

I glanced down at my abdomen. "I promise you will not be growling for much longer. Just let me help this guy real quick." I sighed as I looked back up and saw the guy fall down. "He probably just forgot where his dorm is or something."

I hustled in his direction. I stopped for a quick second on the curb and glanced down the road before stepping onto the pavement.

Two steps in, I heard my mom's voice ring through my head. *"I don't care if it's a one lane street. You should always check both ways."*

Hmm...

What an odd random thought.

Then suddenly, I was weightless. Floating through the air.

How strange was that?

Only, when I connected back to the Earth, I didn't land gracefully. My body smacked the ground hard. Heat shot through my veins, and everything hurt.

I couldn't move.

I coughed and felt something wet slowly covering me.

Or maybe coming from me?

There was a strange whirring sound.

Then the world went dark, and the pain just drifted away.

3 1

GUILLERMO PÉREZ

I didn't know why I decided to walk around campus this evening.

That's a lie.

I knew I was hoping to run into her. Even though I was pretty sure I saw her in her house as I made my way down here.

Whatever.

Even if I didn't *happen* to run into her, I needed the walk. Sure I'd told Cary I wanted a run, but I really wasn't feeling that energetic. Besides, walking let my mind wander and contemplate things more.

Cary had made dinner tonight, and it was really good. The time with them had been fun.

But then he and Jackson got all lovey dovey. Making eyes at each other while talking about homework.

Don't get me wrong. I had no problem at all with their relationship. In fact, I was happy for them. They seemed to really be in love with each other.

The problem was that I had started feeling lonely. Maybe even a little jealous of what they had.

It was killing me to know that she was so fucking close and yet a million miles away.

Why didn't I just jump on her invitation to dinner?

I was such a fucking idiot.

Nope, hold on.

I promised Cary that I would stop beating myself up. It was a mistake. Now hopefully his advice would work, and I could get a second chance with her.

I was so focused on going over the details of my plan, that I nearly jumped right out of my skin when I heard a strange muffled noise at my feet.

Why was I such a scaredy cat lately?

I bent down and investigated the lump in front of me. I poked what I was pretty sure was a shoulder blade and the mass unfolded a bit. Groaning as it did.

I carefully rolled the guy over and came face-to-face with a nearly identical version of Jackson.

What in the twilight zone hell?!

He groaned loudly and turned to his side, nearly vomiting on my shoe.

When I realized how different his hair was, it hit me. This had to be Jackson's brother. The twin he'd kicked out of the house.

Well, fuck.

I knew Jackson said they didn't have a good relationship or whatever, but I couldn't bring myself to just leave the guy out here. Even if he was a dick to his grandparents.

I bit my lip as I tried to remember if Jackson said which dorm his brother moved into, but I kept coming up blank.

Okay. *Think*, Meemo.

What if I took him to the house, and then Jackson and Cary could help get the guy sorted?

Yeah. I'm sure Jackson would appreciate me not just leaving his brother out here like a corpse on a lawn. I would hate to leave him and find out later that he'd overdosed or something.

I reached down and helped Joe or Jon or whatever the fuck his name was, stand.

Once I had him on his feet, I made every effort to ignore the guy's shorts. They were thin to begin with, but the guy rocked a serious boner. What the hell was he on?

"Come on, dude. Your brother can help get you sorted out."

We began walking back to the house, with him shuffling his feet and me holding most of his weight.

Hopefully Jackson wouldn't be too angry at me for bringing him to the house.

I was sure it would just be a simple task of helping him get to his dorm.

If I would have actually remembered my phone for once, I could have just called.

Oh, well.

Maybe the walk would give this guy time to adjust and clear his head a little.

32

GRAYSON LEBLANC

*Y*ou know when you wake up from a dead sleep and you walk all sluggish to the bathroom because you really have to pee, but your mind is still groggy, so you secretly hope you are peeing in the toilet and not like the trashcan or something?

Yeah, that's where I was at.

Not the bathroom.

And I really hoped I wasn't peeing.

Actually, I was currently walking down the sidewalk. Well I say 'walking' but it's more like an assisted standing drag thing.

The guy helping me was *huge*. He looked familiar, but I couldn't quite focus on his features, so I wasn't really sure who he was.

I kept blinking my eyes, but that didn't help clear anything up.

Why did I feel so cold?

I managed to bring a hand to my chest, and connected with solid skin.

Okay? I was shirtless…

What the actual fuck?

My mind wanted to panic that this guy could be like an organ trader for the blackmarket or some shit, but my heart was pumping so slowly that I just couldn't manage to get myself worked up.

The guy must have felt me fidget because he finally spoke up.

"Don't worry. We are almost at your brother's house."

Oh good. Not an organ trader. And he was bringing me to my brother's house. That's helpful.

Hold the fuck up…

I didn't have a brother!

Why would he think I had a brother?

I opened my mouth to ask him just that, but it felt like I had a mouthful of sawdust. I started coughing.

The guy stopped and patted me on the back.

Okay, definitely not an organ trader.

Unless he was trying to keep me healthy so he could harvest my precious organs while I was still alive?!

I dragged in a deep ragged breath, but the coughing continued.

Okay. I think I might have been binging on the cheesy horror flicks a little too much lately.

Once my coughing was under control, we started moving again.

My head felt so damn heavy, so I let it droop.

That was weird. I didn't remember owning a pair of flip flops like these?

Or these shorts? And why the fuck did I have a boner?

Okay, I think I would absolutely remember getting all these tattoos. And a nipple piercing?!

What the hell was going on here?!

We walked up some steps, and the big guy opened the door to shift me inside.

"Jackson! I need your help!" He called out, making me groan from the way the sounds were playing ping-pong ball in my head.

"What is it?" A tattooed, buff guy, wearing only jeans came into my view. He was vaguely familiar, but my brain wasn't pulling him from my memory.

What was with all the muscly guys?

Some kind of biker gang?

When he saw me, he looked absolutely dejected. "Oh, Jonathan. What have you done to yourself this time?"

Finally I managed to push some words out of my dried lips.

"Who's Jonathan?" I croaked.

I watched as the two guys shared a confused look.

This night just kept getting weirder.

I just wanted some ramen.

Wait–I remembered… flying?

And then all that pain, before the darkness.

And now…

"Oh fuck."

33

PRESCILLA BENNETT

I sat on the porch after another delicious meal cooked by my moms.

I leaned back, pooched my stomach out and gave a contented sigh.

I didn't think I could ever move out of my moms' house if they continued to feed me like this.

As I hummed in pleasure, I noticed Meemo coming slowly up the street. And he was supporting... Jack's twin?

They stopped as the guy had a bad coughing fit, before Meemo continued kinda dragging the guy along.

What the hell had happened?

I stood slowly, watching their progress as they came up to our houses and then I turned to open my front door. "I'm going to be next door for a while!" I called out.

Without waiting for a reply from my moms, I jogged down the stairs.

I reached their front door just as Jack said, "Oh, Jonathan. What have you done to yourself this time?"

But then the weirdest thing happened. Jonathan asked, "Who's Jonathan?"

I stared in shock as Jack and Meemo exchanged concerned glances.

"Oh fuck," Jonathan moaned. His head fell forward, and a look of horror came over his face.

"What's going on?" Cary asked as he came up behind Jack. "Why are you all standing in the door? Come into the living room." He gave the stink eye to Jonathan, but didn't say anything to him.

I came in behind Meemo and closed the door softly. Whatever was up with Jonathan, I hoped it didn't hurt Jack too much. I had a feeling Jonathan's actions had been hurting Jack for a long time.

When all of us were in the living room, and Jonathan had sprawled out on the couch, Cary sniffed at him and then curled his lip up. "What did you do, Jonathan?"

"I have no idea what Jonathan did," he said. "But I got hit by a fucking car. I think…" His brow furrowed, and he chewed on his lip. "I saw… Jonathan stumbling across the green and went to help him because he looks like… you." He looked up at Jack with even more confusion on his face.

I had to admit, I was thoroughly puzzled as well.

"And then… I was flying. And hurt so much. Woke up when… you helped me up." He looked at Meemo. "Thank you?" He sounded unsure.

I looked at the guys and all of us seemed to be completely uncertain. Bewildered. Weirded out.

"So…" Cary took a deep breath before asking, "If you're not Jonathan, who are you?"

He didn't reply at first. He turned and looked at me, pleading in his eyes. Pain and fear and longing all rolled up in one tangle of emotion.

I recognized that look. I'd seen it in my best friend's eyes every time he'd felt out of control.

Oh, no.

No, no, no.

This was not happening. This was not *possible*.

"Grayson Leblanc," he whispered.

"What the fuck?!" I screeched.

My knees gave out as my eyes rolled back into my head.

And then there was darkness.

Thanks for taking a chance on our very first co-write! Chaos at PolyTech University will be returning in January with Longing & Chaos. *Please check it out, and leave us a review for* Death & Chaos.

ACKNOWLEDGMENTS

First of all, we have to thank our husbands for subscribing to our crazy on a daily basis. Thanks for putting up with a whole lot of shit from the two of us. LOL.

We also want to thank our editor, who dealt with our chaos in stride… and maybe gained only a few grey hairs…

And lastly, we want to thank YOU. You have enjoyed our madness and pushed us to create this world for you. Thank you!!

ABOUT CASSANDRA JOY

Cassandra Joy is an author of adventure reverse harem romances. She's an avid reader of most every type of romance, but loves steamy MM action and one woman being pleasured by multiple men the most.

While Cassandra loves fantasizing about just such delicious stories, she's happily married to a single man. He's the father and manager of her brood of crazy offspring. They also have a fat cat that thinks he's a guard dog.

Sign up for Cassandra's newsletter to get notifications about upcoming books. You can find Cassandra at CassandraJoy.us or on any of these sites:

ABOUT G.R. LOREWEAVER

G.R. Loreweaver is an author of paranormal romance, twisted fairy tales, and so much more. She specializes in the witty-sexy side of menage and reverse harem.

G.R. loves sweary words, gaming, and debating why tacos are the perfection of food.

You can usually find G.R. and her shenanigans on Facebook in Loreweaver's Literary Lair. More information about G.R., her books, and her awesome team is available at GRLoreweaver.com

ALSO BY CASSANDRA JOY

CJ'S NEIGHBORHOOD SERIES

Dawn of a New Day

A Touch of Sunshine

Out of the Fire

Second Chance at Romance

QUICKIES IN CJ'S NEIGHBORHOOD

Dark Glimmer of Hope

Christmas Lights

Long Awaited

Summer Fun

The Fucked Up Fucking

Christmas on the Range

CHAOS AT POLYTECH UNIVERSITY

(with G.R. Loreweaver)

Death & Chaos

Longing & Chaos

Lust & Chaos

Trial & Chaos (March 2023)

Love & Chaos (April 2023)

AX TO THE HEART

Finding His Heart

Finding His Mage (June 2023)

Finding His Forever (September 2023)

ANTHOLOGIES

A Whale of a Time

Playing for Keeps (August 2023)

ALSO BY G.R. LOREWEAVER

NOCTIFER WITCH SERIES

Noctifer Magick

Noctifer Soul

Noctifer Heart

Noctifer Legacy (January 2023)

CHAOS AT POLYTECH UNIVERSITY

(with Cassandra Joy)

Death & Chaos

Longing & Chaos

Lust & Chaos

Trial & Chaos (March 2023)

Love & Chaos (April 2023)

A MYTH OF DIRE CONSEQUENCES

A Story of Lust & Deceit (May 2023)

ANTHOLOGIES

Once Upon an Ever After

A Whale of a Time

Lunar Rising

Celestial Awakening (June 2023)

Saved by the Every Day Hero (August 2023)

Made in the USA
Columbia, SC
22 January 2023

75737149R00089